Hoping for Treasure
A *Sequel to* On Cue

By Bettie Boswell

Zion Ridge Press

Books Off the Beaten Path

www.MtZionRidgePress.com

Mt Zion Ridge Press LLC
295 Gum Springs Rd, NW
Georgetown, TN 37366

https://www.mtzionridgepress.com

ISBN 13: 978-1-955838-67-2

Published in the United States of America
Publication Date: July 1, 2023

Copyright: © Bettie Boswell 2023

Editor-In-Chief: Michelle Levigne
Executive Editor: Tamera Lynn Kraft

Cover art design by Tamera Lynn Kraft
Cover Art Copyright by Mt Zion Ridge Press LLC © 2023

Dedication

This book is dedicated to all the women who have gone through the loss of a child. I never knew how many others went through similar events until I had more than one miscarriage and discovered relatives and friends who had kept their experience silent. I pray for healing for those who still mourn, knowing that God will take care of our little ones we never knew.

Acknowledgements

My parents' short romance after World War II served as inspiration for Betsy and Dale's story. My grandparents did take in boarders during that time period and some of the layout of the interior of the Woodson House in this story is reminiscent of my happy summer visits at their home. There is a real Underground Railroad building in Sylvania, Ohio, that inspired the Woodson House. That place is the Lathrop House with a hidden room in the basement. As always, I am indebted to my husband and family for their encouragement and patience during my writing endeavors. A big thank you goes to critique partner Ann Cavera, ACFW Scribes Group #201, and my publishing team, Michelle Levigne and Tamera Kraft at Mt. Zion Ridge Press.

Thanks to all the readers who stuck with me to read this trilogy of stories:

Ginny and Scott's musical production, *ON CUE*
Samuel, Missy, Early, and George's experiences on the Underground Railroad, *FREE TO LOVE*
And now Betsy and Dale's WW2 romance that all overlapped in Ginny's little town called Forest Glen.

Chapter One

Ginny
Present day, January

Screech! Ginny cringed as Scott, her husband for all of ten wonderful days, tried unsuccessfully to guide her grandmother's ancient desk through the door of their home. James, a mutual friend, paused and set the end he held onto the porch. They waited while Scott tried to push the now slanting midsection of the desktop back into place.

Ginny bit her lip and clasped her hands. The treasured antique was her inheritance from Grandmother Stuart. It had been the place where she'd drawn pictures, written poems, and held tea parties with her uncooperative brother during summers at their grandmother's home. Research papers for her successful musical, *Incident at Woodson House,* covered the oak piece during the last year-and-a-half. The idea of destroying the old writing table during the move brought a shimmer of tears to her eyes.

Worry involuntarily escaped as she blurted, "Please tell me you haven't broken my desk."

"Don't worry, sweetheart. A weight shifted inside the desk, and it's doing something strange to the structure." Scott bent at the waist and ran his hand across the separating wood. "There are grooves in the top. I didn't notice them when we started moving this monstrosity. I think it will be all right."

She cringed as 'monstrosity' crossed his lips and bit back a comment of her own about respecting history. Their marriage was too new to start a fuss over an accidental slip-up. At least he was attempting to edge her precious furniture through the door.

Scott leaned farther over the desk. "It looks like I can push everything back together." He pounded his fist like a hammer and tapped the slanting wood back into place. "I think we're good. James, lift on three, and we'll head into the front room to your left." Scott signaled and both men groaned as they hoisted the desk through the doorway and into the room Ginny and her brand-new husband planned to share as a study.

Once the men left to retrieve more of her boxes from the rental truck, Ginny smiled as she ran her hand across the smooth oak surface and looked around the study. The space would be perfect for organizing her fourth-grade lesson plans and possibly doing more creative writing. After the success of her musical, the urge to write grew within her soul like a blooming flower.

During their Christmas holiday honeymoon, Scott complimented Ginny's ability to write when they attended a musical at a theater near their hotel. He mentioned that her play, which brought them together, was much better than the one they'd watched. She'd been too distracted to care as they snuggled in their seats during the enchanting time.

Her nail caught on one of the fresh grooves in the desk's top. She leaned closer to inspect the marred surface. She hadn't noticed the break before since papers normally covered the table. Curious, she pushed down and back on the middle section outlined by the grooves.

The desk growled with the sound of a mechanism needing oil as the top moved up and a compartment lifted. The open space revealed an ancient typewriter. A box, held closed by a ragged strip of cloth, sat wedged next to the machine. The scraping sound reminded her of Jezebel's howls whenever the dog heard the chow bag open. The urge to yowl with glee coursed through Ginny as she pressed down a few of the typewriter keys. She should put some paper in the thing and see if it still worked. Maybe there would be some scrap paper in the box. The tattered cloth ends easily pulled the makeshift binding apart.

Ginny took off the lid, revealing what looked like a typed manuscript and a string-bound collection of handwritten papers. A shiver made its way down her spine as she tugged on the bow holding the packet together. She unfolded a few of the pages, revealing poetic writing.

The penmanship on the yellowed sheets seemed all too familiar. How did her grandmother end up with what looked like poetry by Missy Hollings? The poetess was part of the Woodson family she'd researched when writing her musical. Missy's aunt had been married to the original builder of the Woodson house, and they'd provided a hidden room for people fleeing slavery on the Underground Railroad.

She separated more poems from the packet and searched for confirmation of the author. It only took a moment to spot Missy's name on one of the pieces. The paper bore a much later date than the ones in the journals and poetry used in researching the musical. The investigation into the woman's life led to a dead-end after she arrived at Woodson House. The last journal entry revealed Missy helping her aunt with the Underground Railroad. The other writings Ginny explored indicated an interest in a widowed newspaperman named Samuel.

Ginny often wondered if Samuel's attraction to Missy enabled him to overcome the memories of his first wife. Perhaps reading these poems would hold the answer. Since she and Scott were married, she hoped others would also find their true love, or in Missy and Samuel's case, had found theirs. A newer piece of lined paper, like the pages her grandmother used for notes, fluttered to the floor. Maybe it would explain how

Grandmother Stuart came to have the verses. Ginny stooped to pick it up and spotted her name in the salutation.

Dear Ginny,

I made your mother promise you would inherit this desk. You two women are my creative descendants. Knowing your childhood love for working on projects while sitting at this old piece of furniture made me want to share its heritage with you. I never had your gift for words but wanted you to know something about one of your ancestors.

When I was much younger, I made a rough attempt to tell your great-grandmother's story in these typed pages. My writing will reveal how she came into possession of this old desk and the delightful packet of poetry. An elderly employer gave her both items. By now I hope you have gotten over the past and found your true love. After all, this desk needs a creative child to inherit it when you are old and gray like me.

Hugs and kisses to my sweetie,
Grandmother Stuart

Ginny held the letter closer and could almost imagine a lavender scent wafting from the page. She closed her eyes for a moment and pictured the sweet image of the pleasantly plump woman who brightened her childhood with cookies and crafts. Her eyes popped open when Scott entered the room and wrapped his arm around her shoulder while setting a packed box on the edge of the desk.

"Hey, I've never seen one of these old typewriters up close. Looks like this desk held a hidden treasure for you."

"More than one... In addition to the typewriter there are two treasures for me to explore, once we get all of my things moved in." Ginny waved the pages his way and then placed the poems and papers into the box and set it back next to the typewriter. "We'll need to oil the hinges for this hidden compartment." With a grinding squawk, she pulled the desktop into place and watched the ancient keyboard drop back into hiding. "Right now, the priority needs to be getting as much unpacked as I can and prepping for the second semester at school. It's hard to believe school will be starting up again in two days."

Scott moved closer for a kiss. "Our honeymoon may be over but now the blessings of being together will begin. We can work side-by-side on our lesson plans. Or you could always write a book based on your research." He waved one hand toward his own desk on the opposite wall of the room. Then he pulled her in for another peck on the cheek.

Her giggle broke into the moment. "How romantic, side-by-side lesson planning."

She rolled her eyes before melting into his embrace. They'd come so far, from being unwilling partners in the musical's production, to a winter wedding with a happily ever after. However, she could think of better things to do at the moment than schoolwork.

Yips and howls from Carlos, the chihuahua, and Jezebel, the basset hound, pulled them apart. The distant voices of her mom and brother talking with James filtered in from the front porch. They'd arrived to help unpack and return the honeymooners' pets.

"It sounds like the troops are here." Her hand slipped into Scott's as they went out to greet their family.

Mom gave her a hug, before holding her at arm's length. "You look beautiful, sweetheart. Married life seems to agree with you."

"It does, Mom. So, when are you and your guy going to tie the knot?" She winked and pulled her mother's left hand closer to inspect the sparkling engagement ring. Mom finally gave in to her long-time friend's pleas and accepted his proposal. Roy's kind spirit proved his faithfulness and loyalty to her mother.

Her brother Nathan cleared his throat and Ginny turned to give him a side-hug as he tried to balance two boxes.

"I'm happy for you, sister." His elbow poked her in the ribs, making her jump like she did as a kid. "My car is stuffed, like a Christmas turkey, with wedding gifts from your bungalow. Where do you want them stashed?"

"Put them in our formal dining room for now." Ginny's voice lilted into a snobbish accent before she snickered and lifted the top box from his stack. She set the container down to get a better grip. Jezebel gave the package a sniff before licking Ginny's hand. She gave her dog a pat, grabbed the box, and started down a long hallway.

"How formal are you going to be, sis?" Her brother hadn't fully explored Scott's house before. His head swiveled, taking in one room after another as Ginny led him through the historic home. The two dogs padded along behind them, exploring their changed environment. "You won't be hurting for space here. Maybe I'll have to move in with you guys."

"Not a chance, but I'll give you a good deal on renting my old place if you're interested. I'd hate to see my little yellow bungalow get torn up by someone who didn't care about it."

"I've enjoyed hanging out there while you two were away but I'm more into apartment life for now. There was a woman who stopped by and asked about renting the place. Her name was Loretta Luterman. She said she worked at the college and knew Scott from the arts department and church. The lady was really nice, except for her overpowering lilac perfume."

Nathan wrinkled his nose before continuing down the hall. He stopped in front of one of the windows, framed in stained glass. Colors danced across his face in sunlight brightened hues. "Guess we better get busy putting the rest of your stuff inside. The weatherman says we're going to have a blizzard next week."

~~~~~

The predicted weather blasted into town on Wednesday afternoon. Ginny trudged to her car after school and brushed a couple of inches from her windshield. The forecast suggested several days of increasing precipitation, high wind, and low temperatures. When the principal announced snow days for the rest of the week, her fourth graders jumped out of their seats and danced around the room. It took several minutes to get them calmed down enough to pack and head out the door to snow-covered buses.

Once her car windows were clear, she put the vehicle into slow motion and plowed through the slush-covered roads. Thankfully, they didn't live too far from the school. Her shoulders tightened as she traversed what should have taken five minutes, but instead took twice as long due to slow-moving traffic and untreated side streets.

She breathed a sigh of relief when she pulled her sedan in next to Scott's SUV. Her knight in snow gear waved from the sidewalk where he leaned on a snow shovel. Barking came from the front window where two dog noses made mists on the beveled glass.

She pulled her loaded tote from the car and made her way to where Scott worked. "Hi honey, I'm home." She smirked, before welcoming his chilled kiss. Her laughter broke their contact. "I hope our lips don't get frozen together like in the movies."

"Stuck together for a kiss would be okay by me." His chin rested on the top of her head as they wrapped arms around each other and did a slow dance in the snow.

She leaned her head back with a giggle. "But then I wouldn't be able to grade my papers during this week's snow days."

"I heard you're off. We'll see what happens at the college. Most of the students live on campus, which means the college president rarely calls off classes. What will you do without me while I trudge through the snow to do my lectures?" His drama professor's comical expression made Ginny hold her heart with a dramatic flair as they stepped apart.

"You mean besides grading papers and unpacking boxes, or shoveling snow?" She hefted her bag from one shoulder to the other before taking a backward step toward their front door.

"Checking student work doesn't sound fun. Maybe you should explore the treasures you found in your grandmother's old box in the desk." Her sweet husband shoveled another mound of snow from the
~~~~~

walkway and tossed it to the side. "To be honest, I'm kind of curious what you'll find. Regardless, you should enjoy yourself on your snow days."

"Actually, I've only got about two hours' worth of grading, so maybe I will enjoy my time off with some old-fashioned entertainment." She set her bag on the porch and picked up a handful of snow. Packing it carefully, she threw it straight at Scott's chest, to kick off some snow day fun.

~~~~~

The next morning, Ginny stretched and slid the last graded paper into her bag, which sat beside their bed. Lifting a muffin from the plate sitting on her husband's empty pillow, she pulled her covers higher, missing his warmth. The masculine scent of his favorite soap still floated in the morning air. The fragrance mixed with the cinnamon spice emanating from the raisin-filled treat she now savored.

He'd brought her breakfast in bed, before leaving to walk to campus through blowing snow. Scott played his bid for sympathy to the hilt. He'd compared his trek to an ancient ancestor walking miles to school in howling blizzards for weeks on end. The wind moaned a little, but his walk was only a two-block march through the snow.

Rustling sounds came from the dog beds across the room, letting her know Jezebel's sniffer had awakened to the smell of the muffin crumbling open. The thumping of padded hound paws and clicking chihuahua nails drew near as they crossed the room. She stuffed the last of the muffin into her mouth just as the animals began to tug at the draped edge of her blanket. Her day off would include keeping the two pets entertained.

Ginny climbed out of bed and took a quick shower. Afterward, she pulled on a warm sweater and jeans before feeding the dogs. Following a quick romp in the falling snow, the dogs were ready to come in. Jezebel shook enough flakes off her back to make a mess on the kitchen floor. Carlos shivered until Ginny wrapped him in a towel she'd tossed in the dryer for a couple of minutes. Once he warmed up, she used the same towel to wipe the floor. Then they all headed to the study.

A tube of white grease sat on one side of her grandmother's oak desk. The hidden compartment sat partially open, with dabs of the oily substance covering each hinged joint. Scott must have gotten up much earlier than she'd realized and had second thoughts about working the squeaks out while she still slept.

Ginny pushed the contraption up and down while the two dogs howled along with the high-pitched racket. Within minutes the mechanism worked perfectly. She left the typewriter sitting in the open cubicle and pulled the lid off the box full of treasured words. Sinking into the loveseat they'd placed in the study, she opened her grandmother's manuscript and started reading the dedication.
~~~~~

To my reader:

My mother, Betsy, often told me stories of her life as a young woman who lived through the Depression and World War II. Though I have no desire to be an author, I am going to attempt to tell her story as best I can, perhaps in a way my children and grandchildren will find entertaining, in a novel setting. Though I may fictionalize some of the events, I pray you, hopefully one of my dear descendants, can enjoy the stories I loved to hear as a child.

Elsie Stuart

Chapter Two

Betsy's Story
by Elsie Stuart

Betsy
1946

"I'm going to wring your neck, you dumb old cluck." Betsy McCollum's frustration mounted as she chased the errant rooster around the yard. At moments like this, she wondered why her employer still held to the old-fashioned idea of chickens in the backyard. The end of the second World War changed everything. Factories and grocery stores could provide plenty of food, both frozen and canned. Surely elderly Miss Woodson could soon see no more need for the victory garden covering half of the spacious backyard and the raucous crew of squawking chickens, now swarming away in confused masses as she pursued the young male around the slippery pen.

"Bwack, bwack." The taunting rooster crowed merrily as Betsy chased him into a corner. The results of the hard pursuit began to affect the loose bun, once neatly secured at the nape of her neck. Pins and long curls flew in every direction. Creeping forward, she lunged for the malicious bird, only to watch it fly over the fence and directly into the arms of a passing stranger.

Oh my! Not just any stranger. It was one of the soldiers recently returned from war, dressed in full uniform, and quite handsome. Betsy's mouth formed the 'Oh' taking shape in her thoughts, but nothing seemed to come out. She stared at the wavy raven hair and the ruddy, clean-shaven face of the tall man. When her dazed mind fully registered the khaki uniform and duffel bag at his feet, she forced her gaping mouth shut. Memories of another soldier and another time reared their ugly heads. She reined in her galloping thoughts and firmly planted her mind back on the runaway fowl the muscular fellow so easily captured.

The man stared into Betsy's face and wordlessly grinned at her as the squirming bird pecked at the buttons on his uniform. His warm brown eyes brightened as he lifted the crowing cock by holding its backside with one hand while wrapping his other hand around its two feet. "Here's your bird, ma'am."

Betsy stiffened. *Ma'am?* The war might have made her an old maid by some standards, but this stranger did not need to remind her she was in her late twenties and still waiting for a man to notice her presence. Standing tall and smoothing back her hair as best she could, she forced her voice into a reasonable pitch while she fisted her hands at her sides. "Thank you, sir," with an emphasis on *sir*. Betsy lifted her hands but couldn't make them reach for the rooster.

"Glad to be of assistance, ma'am… I'd be right happy to wring his neck if ya want."

There it was again, this time in a pronounced drawl with *ma'am* drawn into two long slow syllables. Strike two. There was no way in heaven Betsy would consider a country bumpkin, even if he was her last chance. She'd grown up country and had no desire to return.

Where did those thoughts come from? She might still be single, but why would her thoughts turn to marriage, especially to someone in uniform who probably had a corncob pipe-smoking mama. He most likey had a whole flock of flapping hens and roosters at home.

"No, thank you. I'll take care of him myself." Trying to hide her disgust at the thought of killing the irritating creature, Betsy reached out for the rooster, who had managed to settle down to a complaining squawk in the man's khaki-clad arms.

Raised eyebrows implied he realized her reluctance to do in the fowl, which made Betsy even more determined to take the wicked creature away from the soldier with the teasing brown eyes. As she grabbed the legs and neck of the wriggling bird, her arms brushed the soldier's sleeves, and Betsy reacted with a shiver. A strange feeling shot through her body. It wasn't a totally new feeling. She knew it all too well from reading Grace Livingston Hill books. There were many of those novels stashed in the bottom of her bookshelf in Miss Woodson's spare room, where she'd lived for the last ten years.

Betsy spent many a Friday night staying up until midnight to finish a good romance. Granted, some of Hill's heroes weren't rich, but by the story's end, they managed to have enough to get by on and sweep the girl off her feet with their undying love. This hillbilly's offer to wring the rooster's neck didn't compare, but the feeling currently coursing through her veins, brought on by his good looks, said otherwise. Heat sprang into her cheeks. Could she embarrass herself any worse?

Betsy shrugged away his help and marched toward the back stoop of the Woodson House. She'd resist this hero. The rooster pecked her hand.

"You're a tough bird, but I'm tougher. We're having roasted chicken tonight." Laughter followed her as she rounded the corner of the house and prepared to take her first step in dinner preparation.

~~~~
~~~~

An hour later, Betsy placed the plucked bird into the speckled blue graniteware roaster along with potatoes and carrots. Pushing the whole thing into the electric oven meant she might be able to catch up on Miss Woodson's correspondence. For a woman in her eighties, her employer produced plenty of letters to post, and errands for her hired assistant to complete. Betsy had been happy to be the older woman's companion for the entire time she'd worked at Woodson House.

She'd been disappointed when the Depression years forced her employer to take in boarders and release the kitchen help. She'd stayed on without wages because the position provided a comfortable bed and more provisions than her parents could eke out on their farm during the lean years. The house became her home in more ways than one. Miss Woodson felt like an old maid aunt. Even the matron's niece, Lottie Woodson Franklin, who helped find boarders, became more like family than her busy parents.

Climbing the steps, she passed one of the boarders who'd moved into town to work for the factory erected during the war years. "Hi, Margie, I'm surprised you aren't at work today."

A cloud seemed to pass over the woman's eyes. Her hands went to her hips. "Some of us girls got cut back to part-time after the war ended. I'm gonna miss my full pay at the office, but the boss says we've gotta open places for the soldiers coming back home. Our grannies may have gotten us the vote, but we sure don't get the equal rights when it comes to work."

"I'm sorry. If there's anything I can do, let me know."

"June's in the same situation with her factory position. Do you think you could influence Miss Woodson to let us share a room to save on rent?"

"I'll see what I can do. By the way, I started a rooster and some potatoes and carrots for supper. If you and June want to help prepare the rest of the meal, I'll ask if payment for the work can be deducted from your boarding fees, since there hasn't been a regular cook in a while."

Betsy hoped her promised exchange would be the case. She'd be glad to hand the cooking chore over to Margie and June, who would be much happier prepping chickens for the table. When she reached the top of the stairs, she opened the door to her small room. Her cot-width bed sat snugly under a sunny window, doubling as both a couch and sleeping area. A large desk, several bookcases, and a set of wooden file cabinets dominated the rest of the space. She felt thankful to have a small closet for storing her meager wardrobe.

A stack of handwritten notes, scented with Miss Woodson's rose water, sat on the corner of the desk. Betsy pushed down on the desktop, and the hidden typewriter lifted into place. She sandwiched a sheet of carbon between two pieces of clean paper before inserting them into the shiny machine and twisting the side knob. The clicking of cogs moving the paper into place always made her anticipate the clear typed words that would soon appear. She flexed her fingers and prepared to tap hard on the keys to make the carbon leave an impression on the extra paper. Miss Woodson liked to keep records of all her notes, even those to friends and family.

The first letter would go to an old friend regarding an upcoming stay by the woman's son, who'd found a job in town. It looked like the gentleman in question would be arriving any day. Betsy wondered where they'd have room for another person in the house. Maybe if June and Margie did move in together, there would be a bed to spare. She finished the letter in no time, accompanied by the pleasant sound of a ding at the end of each margin, reminding her when to hit the return lever and start the next line. Before going to the other correspondence, she made her way downstairs to Miss Woodson's room.

The older woman greeted her with a smile. "Welcome, dear. Did you finish the typing already?"

"I have part of the typing done, but something came up and I need your approval. I noticed you are having your friend Ruth's son come here as a boarder. I wondered where we're supposed to find a place for him."

"Isn't the room above the kitchen available? I thought it opened up recently." The woman looked puzzled.

"The room was available for a while, but you rented it several weeks ago to some newlyweds." A twinge of jealousy wriggled into Betsy's heart. So many couples had reunited after the war. She would never know their kind of joy since...

"Oh my, you are right. I haven't noticed them around much." The matron frowned. "I seem to be getting a little forgetful these days." Miss Woodson laid her knitting to the side and shook her head, looking dismayed.

Betsy wrapped her arm around the other woman's shoulders for a moment and then stepped back. "I do have a possible solution to solve the problem. June and Margie's jobs have been cut to part-time, and they wondered if they might share a room to save expenses." Betsy leaned over to retrieve the ball of yarn when it fell from her employer's lap. "Then one of their rooms would be available for the young man."

"Excellent. What would I do without you?" She lifted her nose in the air and sniffed. "Do I smell chicken roasting?"

"Yes, you do. I did my best to get him started, but I'm thinking it might be good if June and Margie could take over preparing the evening meal as a way of earning some of their keep."

"Their cooking might be a welcome change, no offense to your wholesome morsels." Both women chuckled as Miss Woodson resumed her knitting. Betsy knew how to fix plain, healthy food. However, the few times the other women helped with the meals, there'd been an added charm and flavor that hadn't been there before. She should probably ask the other girls what spices they used.

Betsy stepped toward the door. "I better get back to typing your letters."

"Wait." At the urgency in Miss Woodson's voice, Betsy paused by the door and faced her employer. "I have something you might like to read, besides the novels in your room." The older woman put her knitting aside and walked to a tall dresser. She reached into the top drawer and pulled out a packet of papers bound with a ribbon. "I know you've enjoyed Grace Livingston Hill's books about romance. These poems tell the story of my mother's real-life romance. I want you to have them in case something happens to me."

"Shouldn't your niece have them?"

"She has a whole box of my mother's writings tucked away in a closet somewhere. She's a married woman, but I don't think she has a romantic bone in her soul, unlike you. You've been like the daughter I never had. As you work hard to keep me and this old house going, I've gotten to understand your sweet spirit. All my niece wants is her cut of the money coming in from the boarders. Lottie inherited my brother Warren's practical side, not his aesthetic leanings. I told her the secretary's desk is yours as payment for all you've done for me when we couldn't spare money to pay you. When I mentioned giving you the poems, she said I could do what I wanted with them."

Betsy's heart sank into her stomach. "Are you ill, Miss Woodson?"

"No, dear, I just want to set my house in order, so to speak, before this old mind goes totally haywire, which I'm not planning on for a while."

Betsy took the outstretched packet from blue-veined hands and then engulfed her friend in a full hug. "Thank you for this gift of love."

"You are welcome, child. Now, don't let what happened in the past ruin your chance at love in the future."

The sound of someone twisting the front doorbell pierced the air. Betsy tucked the packet of poetry under her arm and made her way to the front entry. The leaded oval glass in the heavy wooden door pictured the warped figure of a man in a soldier's uniform. Her throat tightened as she approached the door and turned the knob to reveal the man who'd captured the rooster earlier in the day. She narrowed her eyes.

"What do you need this time?" She crossed her arms, and the papers fell to the ground.

He bent over with a smile and picked up the packet. "I could use a good chicken dinner if you have one."

Her mouth opened in surprise. The man had nerve. She pulled the poems from his hand and started to close the door in his face.

His hand stopped the door half-way. "My ma, Ruth Nash wrote to her friend, Arabella Woodson, in hopes she might have a room for me."

Betsy clamped her mouth shut and stepped back from the doorway. She gave a curt nod and motioned for him to follow her into the room where she'd left her employer clicking away on her latest knitting project. Out of the corner of her vision, she saw him pick up the duffel leaning against his leg. He walked behind her through the wooden columns separating the front hall from the owner's living quarters.

"Miss Woodson, your friend Ruth's son has arrived. Would you like him to visit you while I check with the other boarders about opening up a room for his stay?"

"Yes, please. Come in, Dale. You've grown up to be a fine-looking young fellow. I think you were running around in diapers the last time I saw you."

Red sprang into the man's neck as Betsy edged her way out of the room, leaving Dale Nash to deal with Miss Woodson's direct chatter. She ran up the stairs. After dropping the packet of poetry in her room, she tapped on Margie's door. When the door cracked open, she found Margie sitting with her friend, June.

"Perfect. I'm glad you're both here. Miss Woodson said you can share a room and help with the meals to reduce your costs."

"Swell. We'll get things moved this weekend." Margie clasped her hands and smiled at June.

"There is a catch. It seems she took in a new boarder without realizing there wasn't space available. We need to move everything this afternoon."

June pulled the kerchief from her hair. She often wore the head covering during her shift at the factory. She swiped it across her forehead. "Do we at least get to choose which room we take?"

Betsy nodded. "I think you two can make the decision since you're doing the moving."

"Let's take June's room, since it is a little bigger, if there isn't a difference in price." Margie gathered some of her belongings into her arms and headed for the door.

"I'll make sure the rent reflects sharing a room when I type up your new agreement. Now, let me help you get things situated." Betsy hoped she wasn't making a mistake by speaking on behalf of her employer.

"So, who's the new boarder?" June went to the closet and lifted out several dresses on hangers.

"He's the son of one of Miss Woodson's friends. It looks like he's fresh out of the military." Betsy's cheeks felt warm as she moved to the bed and removed Margie's sheets from the single bed. They'd made a good decision, since June already slept on a full-sized bed in the room they would share.

June rubbed her hands together. "Is he cute? What does he look like?"

Margie frowned as she gathered a stack of clothing from the room's bureau. "He's probably the reason we're losing half our pay and becoming roommates."

"We'll make the best of it, roomie. Who knows, maybe one of us will catch soldier boy's eye, unless Betsy has already laid claim to the man." Both women turned toward Betsy, who shook her head in disgust and marched from the room.

Their giggles followed her as she made her way down two flights of stairs and dropped the sheets next to the wringer-washer in the basement. She'd run the soiled sheets later tonight or in the morning when they would have a whole day to dry on the line. For now, she needed to search the pantry near the kitchen for a clean set of bedding for the newest boarder.

Chapter Three

Dale
1946

Dale watched the younger woman slip from the room as he half-listened to Miss Woodson gab about his ma like they'd been pals. Ma worked in the woman's kitchen when she was a young soldier's wife. His parents married right before the first World War, and Ma needed a place to stay and earn her keep while his father went to war. She'd enjoyed the older woman's stories about the past, mostly listening in awe. Miss Woodson seemed ancient to her then and way out of her class. His ma had only been the help, but the woman was kind enough to give her a job when she'd needed one. Back then, Miss Woodson's niece, Lottie, and her family occupied most of the rooms while the woman's husband served in the first war. Dale vaguely remembered playing with an older boy named Woody. With the house full, Ma and her toddler had lived in a cozy corner near a fireplace in the cellar. When Ma found out about Dale's new job in Forest Glen, she reminded him about the basement room and about...

"Are you listening, sonny?" His mother's former employer raised her eyebrows.

"I'm sorry, ma'am. I got a little distracted thinking about Ma and me living here in this house. Do you still have her room down in the basement?" His vague memories of early life took place there.

"Not much down there anymore except the wringer-washing machine. It's so much more convenient than the way we washed clothes when I was a youngster. It's a good thing we have a back entrance to the basement so the water can drain out after the laundry is clean. Otherwise, the machine would be making its racket somewhere up here and might interrupt my peace and quiet."

The ticking of a mantle clock made its way to Dale's ears when the woman paused from her chatter. Had only a few minutes passed? Time seemed to have slowed as his thoughts turned to his mission.

"Would you mind if I go down in the basement during my stay, and take a look at where Ma spent her years here?"

"Not at all, though we've made some changes since your mother lived there. I suppose the place might also be special to you." The older woman's eyes seemed to search his face.

"I reckon it is, ma'am." He shifted uncomfortably in his chair.

"So, tell me about your new job, Dale."

"Well, I finished a chemistry degree right before the draft, so I'll be doing some experimenting at the powder plant for now. I'm not sure how long the job will last since the war effort is finishing up. In the meantime, I'm looking forward to boarding here, and hearing more about Ma's years working at your home."

"Consider this your home, since it was at one time." Her welcoming smile warmed his heart as they shared a moment of understanding. Then Miss Woodson looked down to uncross her knitting needles and poke them into the ball of yarn. "Ruth wrote me a letter about you going to college. She was proud of your willingness to work your way through Berry College."

"Ma brought me up to be a hard worker. If you need me to do some chores for you, I'd be glad to pitch in and help any way I can." He turned his head toward the doorway when the patter of footsteps filtered in from the hallway. The young woman who'd greeted him earlier passed by with an armload of bedding.

"I'll give your offer some thought, but for now, you should enjoy the new job and beautiful scenery around here." The older woman winked. They both chuckled. He jumped in his chair when Miss Woodson called out in an undignified voice, "Betsy, hold up and wait for Dale. You can show him where he will be staying."

The footsteps slowed, and the young woman appeared in the doorway. The expression on her face showed little emotion. The flash of pink in her cheeks told another story. Her gaze refused to meet his. She nodded to Miss Woodson and jerked her head for him to follow. He grabbed his duffel and hurried after her. They climbed the stairs to the upper floor. Her full skirt swished in front of his face. Dale wondered if his cheeks weren't as red as Betsy's. When they reached the landing at the top of the stairs, two women bustled across the hallway, carrying clothing and a basket piled high with shoes and other female doodads. One of the women, a tall blonde, smiled broadly, fluttering her eyelashes. The other stared at him like he was her worst nightmare.

He swallowed and wished Miss Woodson had assigned him the room in the basement. He could live in a barracks full of men, but it looked like he'd be under a full-blown attack from the females living in this house. He followed Betsy into the room vacated by the two women. She put most of the stack of bedding in a chair and spread out a mattress pad on the bed. Stepping to the far wall, she unfurled a sheet into the air and across the mattress. He rushed to the closer side and began tucking in the corners with military precision.

Betsy raised her eyebrows but said nothing about his willingness to help as they spread the top sheet into place, stuffed pillows into embroidered cases, and smoothed a chenille bedspread over the sheets.

The lingering scent of a woman's perfume, along with lint from the spread, entered his nose. Dale fought the urge to sneeze. He pulled a plaid handkerchief from his pocket and stifled his reaction as best he could.

"I hope I didn't force anyone from their room. I'd be glad to board in the basement if you don't mind."

"Margie and June decided to share before you arrived. Their jobs at the factory have been cut back since more of the men have come home." Betsy picked up a rag she'd brought in with the bedding and swiped a dusting of powder from the vanity dresser sitting near the bed.

Ma owned a similar dresser where she sat to powder her nose on church days. It was a gift from her second husband after she moved back home. He stared into the mirror and admired Betsy's oval face as she finished her chore. Had she lost a job at the factory? Maybe such a loss would explain her unfriendly manner. A wave of guilt coursed through his stomach. This war changed so many things. Ma understood. Things changed for her after the first war.

He stuffed his hands inside his pockets and turned away to study the room. The tall walls boasted a picture hanging rail tacked about a foot from the top. He moved to one of the walls and looked closer at a framed oval reproduction of a portrait of Jesus. His family brought him up to believe, but several years in the war put a wedge in his faith. Too many friends went missing or died. Ma's letters let him know she prayed for him every day, hoping he'd find Jesus again. She'd sensed his doubts at his half-brother's funeral.

He shrugged and turned back around to find Betsy studying him with curiosity in her eyes. Their gaze held for a moment until she looked away and pulled a key from below the doorknob.

"We ask you to act like a Christian while you're boarding with us. From now on, no woman should be alone in the room with you. Keep your door locked when you're not here, so there's no question about the safety of your belongings. We provide breakfast and an evening meal promptly at six in the morning and evening. If you have any questions, you may address them to Miss Woodson or me, since I am her assistant."

Tension eased off his shoulders, glad she hadn't been a fired factory employee. "Thank you, ma'am. I reckon I'll do fine here, Miss Betsy."

"You may call me Miss McCollum." A frown wrinkled her face as she turned from the room and walked away with her head high.

He pushed the door closed and twisted the key into place. Women sure were hard to understand. He kicked off his shoes, slipped out of the uniform he'd worn for ease of traveling, and into casual trousers and a button-down shirt.

The change washed over him like a cleansing wave. No more military. No more danger. No more missions to complete other than the one his ma sent him on. He hoped her recollections proved true, but only time would tell.

A full sneeze pushed its way out of his head, as the former resident's scents once again infiltrated his nose. Walking to the window, he pushed it high to clear the air of perfume and powder. He sucked in the fresh air and then released a sigh of freedom. If only it were as easy to get rid of the past.

Betsy
1946

Later in the afternoon, Betsy rolled the last sheet of Miss Woodson's correspondence from the typewriter and placed it in the wire basket of completed work. She'd make sure everything got mailed tomorrow since the postman had already stopped by today.

Her gaze roved around the room and stopped at the ribbon-bound stack of poetry once belonging to her employer's mother. The packet sat on her pillow next to a worn copy of her favorite Grace Livingston Hill book. She was halfway through *Lo, Michael* for the third time. She knew the ending, and with each reading cried many tears over Michael's devotion to Starr. It was time to check out something new, something real, since she hadn't found a man who showed any true devotion to her.

As she untied the ribbon, the papers fell across her bed in a disorganized heap. Each set of pages lay folded in half with a date on the outer side of the fold. Some of the dates were newer than others, with no evidence of order. Betsy knew how to organize after working with Miss Woodson for years. She spread the papers across her bed and had sequenced everything, according to date, by the time June poked her head into the room announcing supper.

"Thanks, June. I'll be there in a minute. I just need to wrap up a project real quick."

"Take your time, Sweet Betsy. I'll go make sure our new boarder knows it is suppertime." June practically skipped across the hallway to knock on Dale Nash's door.

Betsy picked up a pencil and finished numbering each paper so her order wouldn't be lost if the pages were disturbed. She cringed at June's reference to an old folk song made popular by Burl Ives in the last few years.

The flirty blonde boarder had purchased a record player with some of her earnings. She eventually added a Burl Ives album, with the song "Sweet Betsy from Pike" to her collection. Betsy grew tired of the references to her name in the song. The tall blonde seemed to delight in teasing her with the lyrics.

It didn't help knowing the name of her former fiancé, Ike, was in the song too. She looked around the room for a container for the poems. Spotting her wire basket, she moved the outgoing letters to the desktop and stashed the sorted verses in it. Later tonight, there would be time to read a little romance. Whether it was *Lo, Michael,* or ancient poetry was a decision for when she snuggled in bed at the end of the day.

Ginny
Present day

Ginny didn't recognize the title, *Lo, Michael,* but she knew what she wanted to explore. Laying down her grandmother's manuscript, she reached for the packet of what she now had confirmed were Missy's writings. A light pencil mark with the number one in a circle drew her eyes to the top of the paper. She touched the number her great-grandmother's hand once placed on the page. She'd never found an actual connection to the Woodson family before. The discovery was special, even though the relationship didn't come through a bloodline.

She unfolded the yellowed paper. The sheet crackled open, revealing the familiar pale ink and curling penmanship that had graced the journal and poems from her previous research. Some of the words were hard to read in her dark corner of the study.

Standing up from the loveseat, she retrieved a lamp left sitting on the floor since the move. Placing it on her desk, she plugged it in and pulled back the bed sheet Scott had put up as a makeshift curtain. Brightness spilled into the room.

Jezebel raised her head as a ray of light reflected on the floor. She padded over and stretched out in the warmth. Carlos joined the hound for a nap after she refused to react to his playful tugs on her long ears. Ginny laughed at the two companions as she closed the desk's hidden compartment and spread the first poem out in the light from the lamp and sun-filled window.

Waiting for Hope

It seems I'm always waiting,
For words of hope or love.
But then another matter comes,
With orders from above.

Our Sam is loyal to the Cause
He travels far and near
To offer help to those enchained,

Who live their lives in fear.

But since a war has broken out
One country now is two.
And where Sam is I'm unaware,
I don't know what to do.

I wish I'd told him how I feel
But doubt he would have cared.
His heart was broken in the past,
By one whose life he shared.

An unrequited love is mine,
His love is in the grave.
So I must carry on the work,
His press is mine to save.

I'll print the news for all to read,
About this Civil War.
And pray one day I'll see my love,
Come walking through the door.

The freedom fight for all mankind
Is mine to do at home.
But doubting fills my heart with angst.
Where has he gone to roam?

He may not share his love with me,
But people in this town,
Are waiting for a word from him,
To take away a frown.

And so our yearning must endure,
Until this conflict ends.
My heart cries out with lifted hands,
In prayers for all our friends.

Ginny sighed. So Samuel was still being stubborn about finding a new love after his first wife died in childbirth. Missy's words hinted about his activities to infiltrate the South by giving help to those in slavery. It wasn't clear from the verses if he'd become a soldier in the newly started war. Missy loved the man, but his heart seemed closed. Pity for Samuel had crossed Ginny's mind when she'd done the research for *Incident at Woodson House.* Poor man, he must have been devastated.

She and Scott couldn't wait to be parents. They both loved kids and hoped to have a child sometime in the next year or so. This old house provided plenty of rooms to share. They'd also agreed to look into adopting other children. As she reflected on Samuel's first wife, a shiver ran down her back. She hadn't thought about giving birth being dangerous. She placed the poem into the back of the packet, suddenly feeling the need to step away from Missy's sad situation.

After giving the dogs a pet, she plopped back down in the rolling chair and lifted her laptop onto the desk. When she opened it, several new emails popped up, including one from Melody. The music teacher at her school recently took over the care of her brother's orphaned twins. The message contained information for Ginny to pass on to a substitute teacher.

Her friend needed another week to sort through legal details concerning her brother and sister-in-law's estate. Melody and the twins had traveled back to the children's home to gather some of their belongings during the Christmas holiday. Once the paperwork was finished this week, they'd close up the brother's house until summer. Then Melody's teaching schedule would be freer to deal with the rest of the transition.

Ginny swiped a tear from her eye as a big sob heaved from her chest. Two sad stories in a short time sure did a number on her emotions. The twins were adjusting well, and Melody seemed to be enjoying her new role as Aunt Mom, so there was no reason to be overwhelmed. Jezebel laid a slobbery chin on her knee and whined. Carlos jumped into Ginny's lap and kissed her chin.

"I'll be all right, guys. I don't know what came over me. Let's go out and play."

Hearing the word "out," both beasts ran for the back door. Ginny thanked the Lord that Scott built a sturdy fence around the backyard before they were married. For the longest time, he'd put Carlos on a leash for each nature call. She sent the dogs outside and joined them after donning a coat, hat, snow pants, and gloves.

They were yipping at one of the side gates. She stepped around the corner of the house and found Scott attempting to open the snow-covered entrance. The wind had heaped a tall drift alongside the house, trapping the entry in its depths. She leaned over the barrier and met him with a kiss. His padded arms wrapped her in love as a thrill trickled down her back, until the dogs pushed between her and the fence.

"What brings you home so early?"

"They called off classes for the rest of the day. Attendance this morning was meager. There's more snow predicted this afternoon. I packed my bag for online classes tomorrow, and thought I'd come home and snuggle with my honey." His wool-covered hands wrapped around her cheeks.

Carlos yapped. Jezebel howled.

"And your hounds? They may want to join us." Paws scraped against Ginny's padded legs.

"I think the hounds might need to take a nap." His eyebrows wiggled.

Ginny winked at her husband as warmth enveloped her freezing body. "Race you inside."

Scott saluted and turned toward the front of the house while Ginny herded the dogs to the back door, using a promise of treats for enticement as she led them to crates for a nap.

Chapter Four

Scott
Present day

Sunset-tinged clouds slanted rays of gold through the windows as they all snuggled on a couch big enough to hold the whole family of pets and owners. Scott claimed the seat next to his sweet wife. The dogs sat on each side, pushing them closer together, making Scott as happy as he'd ever been. They'd declared this room their den, with most of Scott's ragtag furniture surrounding a big screen TV.

Ginny's more feminine sofa and chairs were located in a room near the front of the house, which she'd designated their parlor. He'd laughed at her formal title for the room, but loved making up for his teasing when he erased her pout with a kiss.

Scott wrapped his arm around his wife's shoulders as he surfed through channels and settled on a newscast about the local weather. The scrolling ticker along the bottom of the screen confirmed Ginny's days off and his employer's decision to go digital for the next few days. After the weatherman announced the roads were hazardous and people who traveled them would face ticketing by law enforcement, Scott flipped the TV off and kissed Ginny's neck.

Carlos growled. Jezebel crawled across both of their laps.

"I think they want us to pay them some attention." Ginny snuggled into his side as she attempted to pet both beasts.

"I guess we have been pretty busy getting to know each other." Scott wiggled his eyebrows in his best attempt at playful flirting. "So what did you do with these animals hounding you all day?"

Carlos jumped into the pile and managed to push his rump between the couple while resting his head on Jezebel's back.

"I followed my husband's advice and read from my Grandmother Stuart's treasure box."

"Did you find out anything interesting or romantic?" He smooched her cheek. Carlos licked their faces, resulting in laughter all around. Leave it to Carlos to ruin the moment.

"It's a mixed bag of mysteries so far. One of the treasures was another packet of poetry from Missy Hollings, the woman I researched for the musical."

"How did your relative come across those?" He pulled Carlos away from their faces and into his lap.

"I'll reveal the connection in a minute. First, let me tell you what I learned so far. Missy's earliest poem spoke of yearning for Samuel. He is off to places unknown while she is working to keep his newspaper going. She didn't mention if he signed on with the military, or was on one of his southern missions spreading information to those in slavery."

"I'm glad I got my gal without too much yearning, though I sure missed you this morning, sweetheart."

"You've more than made up for our time away since you got home." A flush flooded her cheeks as she continued. "I did solve one mystery. My great-grandmother worked for a Miss Arabella Woodson as a companion and secretary, during the Great Depression and World War II. I think Arabella was Missy's daughter. Missy married someone with the last name of Woodson. Samuel would be my guess.

"Anyway, Great-grandmother's employer gave her the desk and poems, along with room and board, when they couldn't pay her salary during the Depression years. What I've read so far in Grandmother Stuart's manuscript revealed information about a new boarder moving into the Woodson House with the same name as my great-grandfather. I think I might be able to predict the outcome of their romance, though the man seems to have a secret my grandmother's fictionalized account hasn't revealed yet."

"The story sounds intriguing. Maybe you should read more of it aloud so I can hear the story."

Ginny pulled away from his embrace and padded into the other room. He missed having his arms around his wife. Pulling a throw across his lap provided some warmth, but not the kind he longed for since she left to grab the manuscript. He stared at the dark TV screen.

Over the last couple of weeks, he hadn't once missed having only the drone of the television for companionship. After their marriage, the historical home he'd purchased when he moved to town now overflowed with love and hope for the future. When she returned, he lifted his wife's quilted throw and covered them in a cloud of warmth. He wrapped his arm around her shoulders and she started reading about the past.

Dale
1946

Dale Nash knew what it was like to deal with military men plotting their next campaign, but he didn't have a strategy for dealing with the blonde woman smiling at him from across the dining table. If her fluttering lashes were any indication, she seemed to have her battle sights set on gaining his attention.

At least the brunette next to her wasn't frowning anymore about the cut back in her hours. Her voice sounded animated while she chatted with the couple sitting across the table. Though, she seemed to be avoiding any eye contact with him. Miss Woodson's gaze brightened when her assistant entered the room and settled into the chair next to his. A sense of relief and something else soaked into his soul like a truce in wartime.

He bowed his head and listened as the married man next to him led them in grace. Hope for a future without war flooded his veins as he fought against all he'd gone through during the past few years. *Help me, Lord. I need to find a way back to You.*

An elbow pressed into his side. He opened his eyes to find Betsy holding the plate of chicken in her delicate hands. The scent of roasted meat awakened his taste buds as his lips tightened into what was sure to be a silly grin.

"Thank you, ma'am." He couldn't resist teasing her with the despised address so he could see her reaction one more time.

"The name is Betsy McCollum, sir." One side of her mouth quirked upwards.

So she could give as well as take. He decided to take the risk of using her first name.... "All right, Miss Betsy, then you should call me Dale." He looked down and watched as her hazel eyes opened wide, along with her unadorned pink lips. He grinned at her for a moment before he looked away and lifted the wishbone cut of chicken from the serving platter. It looked like someone had carved the bird into enough pieces for each person to have one small serving. The war rationing effect still seemed in place for this household.

A loud huff sounded from across the room. The blonde demanded everyone's attention. Was her name June? "Isn't it swell to have one of our service boys home from the war?"

The man beside Dale straightened. "I also served, June."

"Yeah, I know, Paul, but you brought your sweetheart with you when you moved into this boarding house." June's red lips pouted. She smoothed her shoulder-length hair with her fingers and looked at Dale again. Her other hand lay over her heart.

A moment of panic washed over Dale. He looked toward their hostess, hoping she'd interpret his gaze as a plea for help.

Miss Woodson winked at him and tapped her water glass. "Thank you both for serving and to our ladies who kept our world moving while you were away. Now, would everyone please keep the dishes moving? I'm in sore need of some gravy."

With the matron's reminder, the bowls once again began rotating around the table. Everyone dug into their meal. Conversations turned to the weather and spring planting of vegetables and flowers.

Dale took a bowl of green beans from Betsy and spooned a serving onto his plate. "My ma used to save envelopes of seeds from her flowers and vegetables each year. I reckon she had a good eye for saving the best-looking posies, 'cause her flowerbed sure grew some beauties."

Betsy stiffened beside him. Maybe it would be better to keep quiet. She appeared to tighten up every time he opened his mouth. He didn't give up easily, for sure.

"Do you have a favorite blossom, Miss Betsy?" He passed a serving bowl full of rolls to Paul.

"I enjoy seeing Miss Woodson's pansies every year. She keeps them in the shade once summer heats up, which make the flowers last much longer." She kept her eyes looking down at her plate as she pushed a green bean into some gravy. A wisp of hair covered her cheek. He fought the urge to push it behind her ear or release the whole bundle of wavy brown hair from the pins holding her bun in place. She shifted her head sideways and stared toward his hand. "Are you going to eat your spoonful of potatoes before all the gravy drips off?"

His gaze shifted to the spoon paused above his plate. Sure enough, gravy dripped all over everything on his dish. Shoving the utensil into his mouth, he turned to the man beside him and asked where he'd served. He learned that they'd both been in the Pacific and saw limited action due to arriving near the time other troops drove out the enemy.

The few things he witnessed were brutal. After living through the last battles on American soil, both men helped hold the islands. They also provided services to their fellow soldiers who kept moving westward. Paul shared about his duties on a crew servicing the plane that delivered atomic bombs to Japan. The man's wife shuddered, and he hugged her close.

Both men agreed their biggest danger occurred from friendly fire. Fellow soldiers celebrated the end of the war by shooting straight into the air, only to have those same bullets fall right back down. Dale had taken cover in his barracks.

"Well, I'm just glad you made it back in one piece." June's voice broke into their conversation as she smiled from across the table.

Paul frowned and crossed his arms. "Several of my friends from back home didn't fare so well."

Dale nodded in agreement. "I still have trouble thinking about the death of my brother, Joseph. He could keep us all entertained for hours with his stories. The enemy took his bright humor away from us when they shot his plane down. His B-52 exploded with the whole crew on board." He glared at the flirty woman. She had the decency to mutter what sounded like an apology and lower her lashes.

Betsy's delicate hand reached out and covered his forearm. "I'm sorry for your loss."

"Thank you." He wanted to say more, but the tightness in his throat closed in. He laid down his fork and pushed back from the table. Clearing his throat, he strangled out, "Thank you for supper, Miss Woodson. It was real nice, but I need to..." He shook his head and stood, feeling the loss of Betsy's comforting hand. He needed some time alone. When he saw June start to rise, Dale glared at her and ground out a "no" before he headed for the door.

As he stepped out onto the wraparound porch, a breeze swept over his body and brought a slight hope for healing to his soul. He sucked in a deep breath of the freshness. Joseph had been his step-pa's favorite son. The dead fighter pilot was their only baby after Ma married a cousin of Dale's birth-pa. After Pa's death, Papa Herbert came to claim widowed Ma and young Dale, to protect them from the world and keep them in the family. At first, their marriage had been out of loyalty to Pa's kin, but it didn't take them long to fall in love and have a son of their own.

Joseph's shiny personality and athleticism overshadowed Dale's tendency toward books and science. They'd been siblings, but there had always been a sliver of jealousy keeping his half-brother from being really close. The division grew into guilt last year when Joseph died at the enemy's hand. Dale often wondered if his step-pa would have been happier if his older adopted son perished, instead of his true firstborn. During the last couple of years, they'd taken in the neighbor's orphaned son, Gene, to help with their chores, but the hole in Papa Herbert's heart still seemed to exist.

Dale walked down the porch steps and headed for the sidewalk leading toward the creek dividing the neighborhood from Forest Glen's small downtown area. The breeze blew stronger across his face, hinting at a coming rain storm. The cooling air helped calm the swirling guilt trying to claim his soul. He'd done his part to serve. Papa Herbert had welcomed him back from the war. The man hadn't said much. The bags under his eyes spoke of a sadness that pierced Dale's heart and made him accept the offer for the far-from-home position in Forest Glen. Ma's encouragement to search Woodson House provided the perfect reason to leave home.

He paused at the bridge and leaned over the railing to watch the first raindrops plop into the creek. Rings formed, pulsing out through the slow stream. The spreading circles reminded him of how blessed he was by the opportunity to board in the home where he'd been born to a widow, torn from her husband by another war. If things worked out, the house offered him an opportunity to bring a little joy to his ma and maybe to Papa Herbert. Dale hoped he would recognize the family heirloom if he found it, since Ma hadn't given him much of a hint.

A strong gust ruffled Dale's hair right before sheets of rain pushed their way through whispering trees, soaking him from head to toe. He lifted his face and closed his eyes, letting the deluge wash away his cares. Ma had a few sayings about showers cleansing away troubles. She was right as rain, as usual, though she'd probably be saying something about him not having enough sense to come out of the pouring water. He chuckled as he trudged back up the hill toward Woodson House. He hoped the back door into the place was unlocked since he'd sure make a mess if he came in through the fancy front hall. The efficient Miss Betsy would probably have his hide.

Betsy
1946

After clearing the table, Betsy decided to work out her frustrations by doing the wash. She needed to do something with her hands, or she'd be tanning June's hide. The woman made a fool of herself by flirting and making offending comments to the former soldiers. Betsy clung to her aversion for men in uniform because of the unfaithfulness of her former boyfriend, Ike. Still, she respected what the soldiers did to fight the enemy. One of her second cousins, Harry, had lost his life during the war. They'd played croquet together at family reunions. She had missed seeing him the last time she visited home.

Betsy picked up a pillowcase and noticed a faint lipstick stain. Grabbing a nearby bar of Lava soap, she scrubbed at the pink mark until her hands ached. The grit from the soap soon erased the blotch from the cloth. After tossing the sheets in, she realized washing the bed linens alone wouldn't make a full load. She might as well add a few of her things to fill the machine.

She climbed the stairs and grabbed her basket of soiled garments from the closet. In the process, she knocked over a stack of postcards stored on one of the interior shelves. A picture of the Eiffel Tower spilled out from the pile. She picked up the card to admire the site. When she turned it over, bitterness tightened her throat. The words spoke of affection from Ike, another flirter.

At the time, she thought he meant the loving words, until she learned about his wandering heart. She glanced one more time at the tower, before shredding the postcard. Dumping the torn paper into her trash can, she turned toward the door with a huff. She carried her laundry basket from the room and down the two flights of steps to the basement.

The addition of her soiled clothing filled the machine. She added Rinso Detergent to the tub after turning on the water tap. Once the clothes were covered, she turned on the agitator. Rather than climbing back up the stairs, she picked up a broom and swept the dusty basement floor. Too bad she couldn't sweep away the damage June did during dinner. Praying for a calm heart, she sang several hymns as she tidied up the basement. Then she heard a groaning sound, making her want to jump and run.

Chapter Five

Dale
1946

Dale circled to the back of the building, looking for the entrance to the basement Miss Woodson mentioned during her dinner conversation. He prayed it would be open as he leaned toward the short entranceway. The door groaned as he gave a tug. The lock held fast, but he thought he heard someone pause from singing "Amazing Grace" inside the building. He rapped hard on the door and called out a greeting. Hearing a soft voice, he replied by identifying himself. The sound of a latch opening, followed by the turning doorknob, assured him help had arrived.

Betsy stepped back from the doorway and led him through a low-ceilinged area and into the inner part of the basement. She stopped him once he rose to his full height, dripping on the cement floor.

"Wait here until I can bring down a dry towel." She bustled off as he took in his surroundings.

The swooshing of an agitating washer-wringer sounded from the area where he'd entered. He must have interrupted her chores. Was there anything the woman didn't do for this household? She'd make a good wife for someone, but not for him since he wasn't looking. Too many guys married in haste during the war, leading to unhappy returns or widows. Not rushing to the altar was another promise he'd made to Ma. He would not be making such an important decision in a hurry.

He scanned the basement, trying to picture what it looked like when he and Ma had lived in the cellar. The low-ceilinged area where the washer sat looked newer. The addition of a room above probably gave rise to the laundry room. As near as he could figure, from what he'd seen at the dinner table, it must be below the new kitchen. The space looked like it also worked well for draining water from the washer. Reason told him where he stood at the moment would've been where he and Ma had lived.

He didn't see any evidence of the old chimney and oven where his mother did her cooking. The heat from the fireplace oven kept them warm and cozy in the basement, according to her. Today, the basement smelled of coal and heating oil for the boiler tucked into a sectioned-off room. A shiver shook his body. The basement coolness combined with the rainwater reminded him of his adventure outside. He wondered why Betsy was taking so long, but he was glad for the chance to take a look around.

He rubbed his arms and began walking along the walls, looking for the opening Ma once described. His heart sank as he realized whoever sectioned off the basement into rooms had covered or destroyed where the fireplace or oven once existed. Maybe he wouldn't be able to keep his promise to her after all.

The sound of soft footsteps descending the wooden stairs drew his attention back to Betsy. She not only brought a towel, she also held his duffle, which he'd yet to fully unpack. Her cheeks flamed red, enhanced by a bare light bulb, hanging above her head from a hand-hewn beam.

"I hope you don't mind, since you left your door open. I saw this on your bed and thought maybe you might find something to change into. You can throw what you're wearing into the washer with the agitating sheets. I'll come back later to finish the rinse and wringing." She dropped his bag on the floor with the towel on top and fled back up the stairs.

"Thank you, ma'am." He couldn't stop the admiration rushing over him until he heard an unladylike snort of disgust from the top of the stairs.

"The name is Betsy, and you can turn off the washer once you've gotten your clothes soaped up."

The slamming of the door, reverberating from the top of the stairs, reminded him of her snooty dislike. At least she'd only used Betsy instead of Miss McCollum.

Intriguing girl. Too bad she didn't seem to think much of him. He'd show her a thing or two. One of the jobs back on the military base had been taking a turn at doing laundry. When she came back later, hanging the clothes to dry would be the only chore left unless he could spot a clothesline on the big front porch.

He recalled a vague childhood impression of toddling between sheets and attempting to climb the porch railing. His mother's overprotective screams for his safety, as he balanced on the rail, had burned the memory into his mind. The recollection seemed to be one of his few memories of this house. Too bad he couldn't remember the location of the oven or fireplace. It would have been nice to have some of its warmth as he slipped out of his wet clothes and dropped them into the churning wash.

The chill faded away once he put on something dry and began pacing around the basement rooms. He entered the boiler area and noticed a shadow of what might be a large stove pipe running from the furnace and into a wall. Could this have been the spot where the old fireplace chimney flue once sat? As he stepped farther into the room, his head brushed against a chain hanging from the ceiling. He pulled the string for an overhead light bulb to brighten the place. Nothing happened, other than darkness continued to engulf the musty room. The sound of someone walking across the floorboards overhead reminded him of the laundry.

He needed to save his search for another time when he could bring a flashlight or lantern down and get a better look at the dark room.

He returned to the laundry area. Opening the back door, he pulled the washer's rubber hose out into the yard so the soapy water could drain from the tub. The scent of wet earth floated in the air, but the rain had tapered off into a foggy mist. After rinsing the laundry and running the items through the wringer, he put the sheets and clothing in a wicker basket. He debated about walking back outside and onto the porch with his load but decided it would be better to go through the house. He secured the latch on the back door and hefted the basket of damp laundry up the stairs. As he elbowed the door aside to where it opened into the parlor, his gaze fell on Betsy.

She gaped at him and his burden. She set aside a packet of papers and laid a blue bound book on top of the pages. "I said I would take care of the laundry. Do you even know how to use a washer-ringer?"

"No problem, ma'am. I mean Miss Betsy. We worked with a machine similar to yours while in the military. Now if you'll direct me to a clothesline, I'll finish things up."

"I guess I should thank you, then. There's a rope line on the side porch for the sheets. You'll find a folding rack in your closet you can put up to hang your clothes on. Uh—there were a few of my things I added to make a full load. I need to grab them."

Her cheeks sure turned a cute shade of pink at the mention of him handling her underclothing. He set the basket in front of her and turned away with a grin as she rummaged through the damp laundry. He studied a reprinted painting of a mountain hanging on a wall covered in flowered wallpaper. Dale waited until she swished by him with her clothes draped over one arm. The book and papers were in her other hand. One of the pages fell to the floor. It was a poem. He spotted words about a soldier going to war. Did a soldier break Betsy's heart? Picking up the paper, he noticed the number two penciled lightly on the top. Without giving the number another thought, he hurried after the young woman.

"You lost something, Miss Betsy."

Scott
Present day

Scott felt his wife sag against him with a soft snore. It seemed he'd lost his listener. His reading must have lulled her to sleep or else the unpacking wore her out. When a gentle peck on her cheek only brought a deep, sleep-induced sigh, he slid his arms under Ginny and carried her to their bedroom. The sound of paws tapping behind them also signaled an end to their pets' evening. Too bad he needed to stay up and figure out the best way to present a complicated lesson tomorrow using the online format.

"Sweet dreams, my princess." Scott bent over and kissed her lips, which responded despite her drowsy state. Her mumbled response sounded like an attempt to say, "I love you." However, he could barely make it out. After tucking the blankets around his wife and giving her one more squeeze, he reached over to turn off the lamp on her bedside stand. Sitting right below the lamp was poem number two on top of the stack of loose papers. Curiosity got the better of him, as he lifted the pages from the stand. Darkening the room, he made his way to the still-lighted study, where he sat and began reading Missy's poetry.

My Soldier at War

Dark times have come to our struggling land.
Young men now march in a soldier-filled band.
It didn't take long for my Sam to sign on,
Leaving this morning before it was dawn.

No words of loving me fell from his lips.
My torn heart is breaking, it fractures and rips.
I'd hoped he would see us as more than just friends
Now I must wait 'til this Civil War ends.

Fighting for freedom is filling his mind.
Underground Railways are now left behind.
What he did in secret is hidden no more,
Out in the open, he'll fight for this war.

Secretly fighting a war of my own,
Though fewer come north from the chains they have flown.
I'll bind up my hopes as I lay them aside,
Seeking to serve as a guide, not a bride.

Knowing his first wife now lies in the ground,
Ties up his heart strings in knots tightly bound,
Which keeps him from seeing my love soft and new.
Praying and hoping is all I can do.

Printing his paper and serving the Cause,
Working with others to pass better laws,
For freedom from slav'ry and for women's rights,
Serving at home while he goes off and fights.

Prayers for his safety and soft'ning of heart
Lift to the Lord as this war has its start.
My soul cries for peace, but the sins of this land
Force men, like my loved one, to take a brave stand.

Standing alone, on my own's for the best,
Telling the news of this war to the rest,
For people who yearn for the news of their kin,
Fighting the battles they're hoping to win.

Scott set the poem aside and steepled his fingers as he reflected on Missy's decision to forge on, despite Samuel not returning her interest. She demonstrated courage to do what needed to be done, despite the lack of a promise for the future. Love for his own wife kept Scott from perusing any more words without her nearby. He'd enjoyed reading the story earlier as she leaned into his side and looked forward to a repeat performance tomorrow. He turned on his laptop and did what he had to do for the morning classes.

Chapter Six

Ginny
Present day

Friday morning came way too early as Ginny sat straight up in bed. The scent of frying bacon wafted through the air. Instead of causing her senses to yearn for a hearty breakfast, her stomach rolled and threatened to give up its contents. Pushing her covers aside, she ran for the bathroom. She hung over the toilet for several minutes, throwing up and releasing dry heaves.

Great, her second good snow day of the year, and she'd picked up the stomach bug. Someone she'd come in contact with on their two-week honeymoon, or one of her students during their first days in class after Christmas break might have shared their germs. A couple of children were missing on Tuesday after being there on Monday. She grabbed a rag and moistened it before running it over her forehead.

Scott's voice rang out from the hallway. "Breakfast is served."

The dry heaving started again. "I'm sick. Take it away."

She heard the rattle of silverware on a plate being set down before her husband stepped into the bathroom.

Scott wrapped an arm around her back and helped her hold the cool rag to her head. "I'm sorry, sweetheart."

"I think I've got some kind of flu. You might want to steer clear for a while." She took the moist cloth and wiped her mouth.

"No worries, honey, the marriage vows said in sickness and health. I guess the flu counts. Besides, I'm pretty sure I've already been exposed." Scott cleared his throat and took a step back.

She hoped he didn't join her at the toilet. "Just get the bacon out of the bedroom. The smell is…" The urge to gag started again.

Scott stepped out of the bathroom. A wave of loss washed over her back. She missed his warmth. The sound of a plate rattling, dogs barking, and a surprised exclamation from Scott reached Ginny's ears.

"I don't think the bacon is going to be a problem. Jezebel and Carlos took care of your breakfast tray while we were in the bathroom. I wasn't thinking clearly when I set it down on the floor. My thoughts were on you being sick."

Leaning against the bathroom door frame, Ginny took in the mess. Laughter shook both of them as Scott took the breakfast tray away and returned with an empty bowl, which he set on her bedside table. "I'll put your poems on your grandma's desk for safekeeping, then be back to help you to the bed."

Ginny hugged her arms around her chest and felt an ache. Great, swelled glands were the last thing she needed this morning. At least she didn't think she had a temperature. Scott rushed into the bathroom and led her back to bed. He wrapped a blanket around her body, turned the lights off, and coaxed the dogs from the room before closing the door.

An hour later, she awoke feeling much better. A quick shower brought a more normal feeling to her tilted world. After pulling on a warm sweater and comfortable jeans, she padded down the hallway toward the half-open door to their study. She thought about stepping in for a good morning hug, but Scott and a student were discussing an assignment over the college's online video program. Her empty belly growled. The urge for some toast or crackers propelled her to the kitchen. She didn't want to think about anything spicy or fried until she knew her stomach would behave.

As the smell of toasted bread made its way into the air, Carlos and Jezebel trotted into the room and planted themselves near the kitchen table. Ginny shook her head. She grabbed her toast and set her plate down on the side of the table she'd claimed as her dining spot last week.

"Don't even think about getting a second course of breakfast this morning, dogs. This serving is all mine." Hunger still gnawed at her stomach after two slices, so she decided to go for a couple more. When she finished all but a few crusts, she gave in to Jezebel's pleading eyes and Carlos's two-legged begging dance. She tossed them each a small morsel.

Leaning back with a contented sigh, her gaze took in the large kitchen of the historic home now belonging to her, and of course Scott. She'd teased him more than once about marrying him for the house. They both laughed, knowing their love meant more than the ownership of a building. The home had been on her dream list for many years. He bought it when she didn't have the funds to consider making an offer. They'd been married three weeks already, two as honeymooners and one as snowbound newlyweds living in the beautiful home she adored. Life couldn't get any better, so why was she suddenly fighting the urge to yawn?

The odor of cardboard boxes scented the air as she tried to breathe deeply. She needed to get rid of the stink coming from one side of the room. She stared at the wall, still stacked with a multitude of boxes marked "kitchen." She knew she'd find more food supplies in the cartons than the few items already sitting on nearly empty shelves.

At least, Scott's refrigerator contents provided a good supply of bread. She'd also noticed a couple frozen meat cuts and vegetable packets in the freezer. They had finished off the last of Mom's welcome home casserole last night. Maybe Mom's dish of food had spoiled and made Ginny ill this morning. She shook off her musings and started pulling canned goods from the closest box.

By the time Scott finished his morning classes and walked into the room, Ginny had transformed the area into her idea of the perfect kitchen. A pot of chicken noodle soup sat simmering on the stove. All evidence of packing boxes had disappeared. Even the cardboard stench that made her feel slightly queasy had given way to the scent of boiling chicken broth. Canned goods, utensils, and pots and pans were now sitting in orderly array in the cabinets.

Colorful kitchen towels and potholders, received as wedding gifts, brightened the room along with a small bouquet of artificial flowers that once decorated the table in her bungalow. Ginny's oak table now sat in their formal dining room since Scott's more casual one fit better here in the kitchen.

Her cookbook collection sat cozily on a small shelf against the wall, recently hidden by boxes. Those volumes included her favorite recipe book from the grandmother who wrote the manuscript found in the oak desk. Next to the shelf, Grandma Stuart's old hutch held a mish-mash of cups, saucers, plates, and sentimental statuettes from Ginny's students and family heritage.

"Someone has been busy. You must be feeling better." Scott's arms wrapped around Ginny as his warm lips covered her mouth with a long kiss. Her knees nearly buckled as she leaned into her beloved husband for support.

Half an hour later, they sat at the table, sipping soup and chatting about his classes. He had one more online meeting for office hours. Then his day would be done.

"I'll turn my microphone off. Unless someone virtually pops in, we can sit for a while with your grandmother's manuscript or the poems, if you would like."

"Reading sounds wonderful, if I can keep my eyes open this time. I wonder if the second poem provides anything interesting about Samuel and Missy."

"I have a confession to make. I took a look at her verse last night. The only thing changed in Missy's verses is that Samuel enlisted in the military. She is still keeping up with the newspaper and supporting women's rights."

They made their way to the study and cuddled on the loveseat with the papers. Ginny scanned the poem Scott read. As he snuggled into her side, she opened to the next page of Grandmother Stuart's story about Betsy.

Betsy
1946

Betsy listened to Margie chatter about how the women should have equal pay for the jobs they'd been doing in the powder plant and other factories around the states.

"Why, look at that Rosie the Riveter gal. She's been on lots of posters and did plenty of work for the war effort. If I was a betting woman, I'd say the odds are they didn't pay her as much as some man who's come back to take her place in the airplane producing factory."

June nodded in agreement as she packed her lunch sack in readiness for her last full day of work. "Though, it would be swell if some soldier boy gave me a little notice. I wouldn't mind staying home and working in his kitchen. Speaking of which, have either of you seen our new fellow this morning?"

"He left before breakfast, grabbed some dry toast, and took off like something or someone was after him. I wonder who might have scared him off." Betsy winked at June as she finished wiping breakfast crumbs from the table. After dropping the litter into the waste can, she began drying the clean dishes using a cloth with red and blue stripes running along each side. As each plate dried, she placed it face down on the table along with a place setting of silverware.

Margie snickered as she leaned over the sink and ran another rinse over the beans they'd left soaking overnight. "You can at least help me this morning by finding the hambone hiding somewhere in the ice box. It will add a savory taste to these beans. They should be nice and tender by dinner." She sprinkled a liberal amount of salt and pepper into the pot. Then she hefted the pot to the stove and turned on the burner. Dipping into the bacon grease container, she dropped a hunk of lard into the soup.

June waltzed over and added the found hambone to the beans. "I should be home in plenty of time to make some cornbread to go with these beans."

"Perfect, since my shift is in the afternoon." Margie swirled a long spoon around the pot.

"Thank you both for taking over the cooking. This will be a help for all of us." Betsy added overturned glasses to the place settings, then draped her drying towel over one of the three wooden prongs above the sink.

"No problem, since we're taking a cut at work. See you two sweet peas tonight." June waved over her shoulder and left the room, with her lunch sack in hand. A whiff of gardenia-scented perfume trailed behind the young woman.

"I'll be in Miss Woodson's rooms helping with her chores, if you need me." Betsy picked up a tray holding a cup of her employer's favorite tea and some sugar cubes.

"Enjoy. I'm going to read through the morning paper until this pot starts boiling and I can lower the heat. Maybe I'll find a lead on another job. I could always try to be a Fuller Brush Man." Margie pointed to an advertisement on the back of the paper.

"I don't think you'd qualify as a man." Betsy set the tray down on the table's edge to have a closer look.

"Of course not. The latest news says the company is looking for female Fullerettes. Though I'm not sure how I'd do selling brushes door-to-door. I do get along pretty well with their products." Taking the circular vegetable brush from the counter, she waved it in the air.

"I guess you will need to brush up on your selling skills." The teacup rattled on the tray from Betsy's giggles as she headed out the door to attend to Miss Woodson's needs.

~~~~~

"Good morning, dear. I'm glad to see you're in a good mood today." Miss Woodson sat at her vanity and ran a powder puff across her cheeks before rising and moving to her settee and side table. "Does this have anything to do with our new boarder? He's such a nice-looking young man, don't you think?"

"Definitely not!" Betsy said. "I have no plans to ever be interested in another soldier boy. If I decide to look for a man, he'll be a city fellow with a stable job."

"I heard Dale has quite a fine job at the plant working as a chemist. His career sounds pretty stable to me." The older woman chuckled. She picked up her napkin, wiped her lips, and then set the cloth back on her lap.

Betsy turned away and wiped powder from the vanity with a dust rag. Steady job or not, she wasn't interested in Dale. Besides, who knew how long the powder plant might stay in business with the war being over? She turned from her chore, tucking the dusting cloth into her waistband.

"I'm sorry Ike Jones hurt you so much. Not every former soldier will betray you like he did." Miss Woodson stirred two sugar cubes into her tea before taking a dainty sip. "This is the first I've heard you say anything about wanting a city man."

"I know what it's like to live in the country. Dale's twangy voice sure sounds country to me, so don't try any matchmaking schemes on me, especially with him. I don't want to have to kill chickens, string beans, and live in a shack all my life. I want something better." Hands on hips, Betsy stared at the woman, who had never married.

"Better than working for me?" The older woman lifted her tea toward
~~~~~

Betsy. She took a full swallow and looked over the rim at her employee.

"No, Miss Woodson. You've given me the best life ever." Betsy stretched down to pick up a few stray hair pins. She placed them in the porcelain container sitting next to Miss Woodson's hairbrush and round powder box.

"But you've been killing chickens and stringing beans for me the last few years." The click of knitting needles signaled the start of Miss Woodson's day.

"I've also learned to do secretarial work and take care of myself without having to rely on any man." She slipped into the bathroom and tossed the dust cloth into a basket of soiled towels.

"Sometimes a fellow can be mighty handy. I heard you received a little help with the laundry last night."

"Help I didn't need. Now, what can I assist you with this morning?" Betsy regretted sounding cross with her boss. She forced a smile to her lips as she straightened Miss Woodson's bed and fluffed her pillows.

"Grab your pad of paper so I can have you write a letter to Ruth. I need to let her know her son has arrived and settled in." A crafty grin spread across Miss Woodson's face.

Betsy slid into her chair, picked up her pencil, and held it poised in the air. Two could play this game. "So how come you never married, Miss Woodson?"

"I guess I never met a perfect fellow who could handle my opinions. I was quite active in trying to get the women's vote back in my younger days. I followed in my mother's footsteps in supporting change for women. Being a suffragette didn't go over too well with the fellows my father brought around as possible suitors. Like you, my parents wanted me to have a rich city man. They thought someone with those qualifications could take care of their daughter and this old house in style." The sound of knitting needles clicking echoed in the room for several minutes.

Betsy searched the room. Her eyes focused on a woman's portrait hanging on one of the walls. "Tell me about your mother. I've read a couple of her poems and would like to know her better."

"You would have liked her. She was quite a woman." Miss Woodson poked her needles into her ball of yarn. She stared at the painting for a moment before speaking.

Betsy's shoulders sagged in relief when the woman started talking about her mother instead of dictating the letter about Dale.

"My mother, Melissa Hollings, ran a safe house for the Underground Railroad during the Civil War, right here in Woodson House. When Mother first came north, an aunt owned this house. Mother went by Missy back then. She left her southern home to free one of her slaves. They traveled with her other aunt from Alabama. Once her maid traveled on to Canada, my mother stayed with her aunts and worked to liberate people in slavery and fought for women's rights." The older woman put a finger to her lips, looking thoughtful.

"There's something of Mother's that I'd like to show you." Miss Woodson moved back to sit on her vanity seat and pulled her jewelry box closer. She sorted through the small collection of pieces until she found a delicate necklace. The teardrop-shaped stones hanging from the intricate web of gold looked like someone connected the semi-precious gems to the metal form using sewing thread. The older woman held the bauble in the air, as a distant look crossed her face.

Betsy laid an arm across Miss Woodson's shoulders and bent nearer to admire the jewelry. "I haven't seen this necklace before. Is it an heirloom?"

The older woman nodded. "This was my mother's lavaliere and my grandmother's before her. Mother never knew her birthmother who originally owned this jewelry. My grandmother passed away when Mother was a toddler. The mother figure who raised her was a woman bound in slavery. She treated my mother and her own enslaved daughter as equals. Later, the two girls escaped to the north to be free from their past. Mother took little of her Southern heritage with her except for this necklace. It broke apart from her childish play in an attempt to be close to her departed parent. Her father said his wife's grandmother owned the necklace during her lifetime. He didn't place any value on it, other than sentimental attachments, so he gave it to my mother for entertainment." She lifted it to the light and fingered the repairs.

"During her journey north, a young girl named Elsbeth, who lived on a canal boat, helped her sew the stones back onto the filigree. Her memory of the child is how I got one of my middle names. My other middle name, Early, came from the young woman who served as her childhood companion. My grandfather eventually revealed the girl was Mom's cousin.

"Miss Early served as Mother's personal maid on the plantation until they fled north to Woodson House. Mother wore the lavaliere on her wedding day and hoped someday I would do the same." She dabbed her eyes with the embroidered handkerchief she kept tucked in the belt at her waist and held the necklace to her chest. "I'd like to wear it today. Would you please help me with the fastener?"

"I'd be glad to help." As Betsy clipped the clasp closed, she reviewed the things Miss Woodson had revealed. The poem she'd read about continuing to work for the Cause now made sense if the poetess worked for the Underground Railroad. "Where did the people running away from slavery hide in this house?"

"Mother never shared any details with me, other than the fact she helped them on their way further north. She also wrote abolitionist poems for *The Gazette*. Mother always wondered if someone would accuse her of being a law breaker, which she was until the Civil War came to an end."

Miss Woodson patted the jewels lying against her chest and then lowered her hand to admire their reflection in the mirror. "This old piece looks pretty good. Maybe I can loan it to you for your wedding day." A mischievous expression crossed her face as she winked at Betsy's reflection before rising and returning to the chair where she liked to conduct business. "Now, let's get a letter started to my good friend Ruth and let her know her handsome son has arrived. If I'm not mistaken, you will have some pretty stiff competition from June, to gain his affection. We'll have to tell Ruth that her son is a good catch for at least one of my girls."

Betsy fought against the urge to roll her eyes. Instead, she picked up her stenographer's pad, taking notes for Miss Woodson's letter to Ruth, regarding her son's safe arrival.

"Dear Ruth, I hope to have something special to tell you by the time you read this."

Chapter Seven

Ginny
Present day

Saturday, after another early morning of feeling queasy, Ginny picked up a pad of paper and started making a list of things she wanted to accomplish for the day. Number one was sorting through the boxes from her bathroom and laundry room. If she didn't find another jug of laundry detergent, they needed to venture outside into the remnants of the snowstorm and do some shopping. Between feeling tired and having to deal with what might be the flu, she had no desire to leave the warm house. Hopefully, she would be better by Sunday. It was her day to greet at her small urban church with her friend Hope.

For now, she and Scott had decided to split their time between the two congregations each of them had attended before meeting during the production of the musical. They both played integral parts in those churches. Scott was active in the praise band when they attended the larger suburban church. Ginny served in many capacities at the smaller church she attended with her mother. Once they started a family, worship habits would probably change, but for now they'd decided to alternate between the two places.

With a sigh, she laid down her pencil and trudged off to the boxes they'd placed near their shared bathroom. She pulled off a strip of tape from the top carton and removed pastel towels and washcloths. The small closet in the restroom provided plenty of space for her collection. Scott's basic set of a few threadbare towels and drab rags looked like they'd be heading to the dust cloth pile soon. She looked forward to using her newer, fluffier ones in the future.

The next container held her feminine products stash. As Ginny sat on the floor placing the plastic wrapped packages on a different shelf in the closet, excitement fluttered in her stomach. They'd been married for three weeks. They'd happily enjoyed their new life together and she hadn't thought of much else outside of her first week back to school. It had been almost five weeks since her last period.

They'd not wanted to wait for a family. Could it be?

"Scott!"

Something in her exclamation must have sent her husband into panic mode. He rushed into the room and hovered over her in a breathless state. "Are you okay? Did you fall?"

Ginny started laughing and couldn't stop. She held up what she'd been shelving. "I don't think I'll need these for the next nine months."

"What are you talking about?" Scott's jaw dropped as comprehension spread across his face. He reached for her hands and helped her stand. "Are you positive?"

"I'm pretty sure, but we might want to get a certain little test from the drugstore." She leaned closer as he wrapped his arms around her.

"I love you. You are going to make a great mom."

"I love you too, Dad. Now let's go to the store."

"It's still pretty slick out there. I wouldn't want you to fall. You stay here and take care of yourself. I'll be right back." As Scott babbled, he stumbled backwards, knocking over boxes of supplies stacked on the floor.

"I hope you can keep your balance when you wade through the snow." Ginny laughed as she tiptoed through the mess and joined him for a kiss.

Scott hugged her close and whispered, "A baby already. I can hardly believe we are going to be parents." A grin spread across his face. Then his expression changed to one of concern. "I'm almost finished putting my information on our papers to be considered for adopting a child. Maybe we should wait to turn them in until after the baby comes."

"I wouldn't worry about the timing. I've heard the adoption process can be very slow. It might be years before a child becomes available." She placed a hand on his cheek.

"I don't know. We did decide we'd take an older child if the opportunity arose. There might be someone who needs us sooner." He rested his forehead against hers.

"Then we will make room in our hearts for them." Giving Scott a nudge toward the door, she returned to sorting the items scattered on the floor. He paused at the bathroom entry and stared at her, appearing to be in a daze. "Go buy the test and get back here as soon as you can. Oh, and we need some laundry detergent. If you see some at the store, please grab a jug."

Scott
Present day

Sunday morning, Scott paced near the bathroom door. Per the box's instructions, they waited to use the test until early the next day. He'd been riding a proverbial rollercoaster since Ginny's exclamation yesterday. Waiting had been difficult. He tossed and turned until his wife went to the closet and retrieved her own blanket to sleep under. Hopefully, he'd be able to share his covers better tonight.

The sound of the toilet flushing and his wife retching resulted in mixed emotions. He was excited about the possibility of having a child, but guilt washed over him as he waited for her stomach to settle. He leaned into the small room to rub her back when she moved to the sink to rinse her mouth. Moments later, he dared to ask the question he'd been waiting for. "What did the test say?"

"It's on the edge of the tub. See for yourself. I've been too busy to check the results." His sweet wife sounded grumpy. He hadn't seen an angry side of her since the early days of working on her musical together. Ginny had been upset when she found out he would be taking over directing her musical.

He decided to try a different tactic. "When you are ready, we'll look together." He stepped back with his hands up in surrender position and waited.

She mumbled a quiet apology and picked up the small plastic strip. A trembling smile lit her face as she held the positive answer closer so he could see. He took the test from her hand and laid it on the sink. Then he wrapped his arms around his wife and child. He was going to be a father.

"I can hardly wait to share the news!" Scott stepped back and held Ginny's hands in his. Her bewildered expression made him pause. "Sharing would be okay, wouldn't it?"

"I'm also excited, but maybe we should wait until we get the official word from a doctor."

"You're right. We'll get you an appointment with Dr. Giles as soon as he opens his doors tomorrow."

Ginny stepped away and crossed her arms. "Some of us will be going to work all day and might need to answer the doctor's personal questions."

He missed her closeness as a chill washed over him from head to toe. "You're right. Sorry if I'm a little too enthusiastic." He said the words of apology, but couldn't contain the pride welling up in his chest as he reached out and surrounded her cheeks with his hands. When he pulled her nearer, she bowed her head at the last moment. He brushed his lips across her forehead, though he'd hoped for a kiss.

"I'm thrilled to be expecting, but maybe we should keep something this precious to ourselves until we know for sure." She stepped away and turned back to the sink with a hand over her mouth.

He gave her a few minutes before he dared to say anything more. Once he heard water running, he opened his mouth. He hoped he wasn't inserting a huge piece of leather to chew on. "So we can't even tell your mother?"

"No. At this point, we definitely won't tell my mother. She wanted us to wait a while before having a baby. She thought we needed time to bond. Mom wasn't happy when I hinted differently. After the failure of her marriage, I think she is concerned about us making the same mistakes." Ginny stepped from the bathroom, looking a little pale except for her pink cheeks. Scott couldn't help admiring his blushing bride and the mother of his child.

"I'm glad she's finally over your father and given Roy a chance." He'd heard how Ginny's father had deserted his family for another woman. The man met a tragic end soon after.

"My brother and I are both happy she agreed to marry Roy. He has been so kind and patient with her for many years. He'll make a super grandfather for our baby."

"Do you think your mom and Roy will be at church this morning?" Scott didn't want to worry his wife but knew Ginny didn't easily fool his mother-in-law. She'd be on their case the minute she saw them, asking if her daughter had been sick.

"Mom attended a book and craft fair appearance yesterday. The event was only about an hour away. I'm sure they'll be at church with a casserole in hand. The annual business meeting and potluck dinner are today."

"Are you going to be able to handle the meal?" Scott watched his wife wipe her face with a damp rag. She attempted a wan smile.

"I should be all right by the time we make it to church. This seems to be an early morning thing. I hope my stomach follows the pattern so I can teach tomorrow."

"Maybe I'll put some baked beans in a pan for our potluck contribution." Scott had forgotten about the dinner, but he figured he could open a couple of cans and throw them in the oven for an hour. He'd do anything for his beloved. Even eat cooking ala Scott.

"That sounds like a good idea. Just add a little brown sugar, ketchup, and cinnamon before you bake it. Please, no bacon, I'm..." She twisted away.

Scott took his cue and headed for the kitchen. If they were lucky, he'd have the beans warmed up before time to head to church. The anticipation of being a father quickly overcame his doubts about his wife being able to keep her secret.

Dale
1946

The scent of butter and warm cornbread entered Dale's nose. Miss Woodson ladled out servings of ham and bean soup over the bread and passed them to each side of the table. The aroma washed over him. He remembered his mother talking about the secret ingredients she used when she flavored her soups.

Secrets... He hated knowing he promised to keep them. His mother had been embarrassed about leaving the item behind when she left for her hurried marriage of convenience. She swore him to secrecy in case he couldn't find what she sought. She didn't want any of the relatives to get their hopes up about finding the lost family heirloom.

Years ago, Mom had been surprised when her husband's cousin came to offer them a home with him. She'd given little thought to any of the past lying tucked away in the hidden room she'd discovered next to the old oven and fireplace.

"You're awfully quiet tonight, Dale." Miss Woodson interrupted his wandering thoughts.

"It's been a busy day. There were many new things to go over at work today." At least, the part about his new job was true. It seemed like eons had passed since he'd worked outside a military setting. The new supervisor was demanding, but mild compared to his last drill sergeant. They'd gone over safety rules for the lab and expectations for the work he'd be doing. It would be a nice job for the time being.

The powder plant hadn't promised anything long-term. He appreciated their honesty and hoped he could find what he was looking for before the factory closed down or changed to producing something that didn't need his skills.

"My compliments to the cooks, the soup and cornbread are delicious. It reminds me of my mother's meals before the war." Dale rubbed his belly.

June fluttered those ridiculous lashes of hers and blushed. "Margie started the soup. I finished everything up. I hope you like peach pie." She looked hopefully in his direction. Though she seemed more subtle tonight, her attraction was still evident. Margie nodded an acknowledgement of his compliment but didn't seem motivated to say anything.

An awkward silence engulfed those sitting around the table.

Betsy cleared her throat. "Miss Woodson dictated a note to your mother letting her know you arrived safely."

"Yes, we told her you were doing well and plenty of sweet young women are here for you to choose from." Miss Woodson grinned as all the younger women turned various shades of pink.

Paul hugged his wife closer. "This one is taken, aren't you, sweetheart?"

"I sure am. I could use some sweet peach pie. I'm eating for two these days." Ellen placed a hand on her midsection.

Gasps of congratulations came from the women. Betsy leaned forward around the two men and asked about a due date. After the expectant mother mentioned a winter month, everyone resumed chatting about their days. June and Margie cleared the table of dirty dishes and passed out dessert plates with pieces of pie and dabs of whipped cream.

Dale swiveled in his chair and gave the father-to-be a pat on the back.

"Congratulations."

"Thanks, man. One of these days maybe you'll be the lucky one, once you tie the knot with a good woman." Paul pecked his wife on the cheek.

"I have to keep some promises to my mother first. Then maybe I'll start looking." Dale had no desire to chase after any of the girls. His half-brother, Joseph left several girls mourning over his demise. Dale never dated back home. He learned quickly that most girls only made friends with him to meet his popular sibling.

"Don't wait too long. There are plenty of fellows looking to settle down after all they've been through in the war. If you open your eyes, you'll see plenty of women who've been waiting for the right man to come home." Paul's elbow connected with Dale's ribs and pushed him into Betsy's side.

When he bumped into her arm, she squeaked. Cream fell from her pie-laden fork and landed with a plop on her other wrist.

"I'm so sorry." He grabbed a cloth napkin and held her arm in his while he cleaned the cream from her hand.

When Dale looked up, he stared at her widened eyes and slightly open mouth. He swallowed and forgot any further words he planned to say. Roses bloomed in her cheeks. A man's laughter broke into his thoughts. June blew out a loud huff of air, making him hurry to finish the task. He mumbled another apology before releasing her hand.

"Can I get you more cream, Betsy?" Margie giggled for the first time in his presence. At least, her animosity from the incident seemed to have faded, for the time being. Though he hoped his actions hadn't built a thicker wall around Betsy. If her blushing cheeks were any indication, his touch made an impression of some kind. He hoped it wasn't embarrassment.

"I'm fine. I've had enough." She scooted back from the table. "Excuse me. I need to finish some things before the sun goes down."

Dale's gaze followed her as she left the room. The sound of the front door opening and closing echoed from the front of the house.

Paul chuckled. "You should go see if she needs something."

June sighed. "You could always help me with the dishes."

"I've got you covered, friend. Now, quit being a sore loser." Margie picked up Betsy and Dale's dessert plates and headed for the kitchen.

"I haven't given up yet." June winked at Dale. "We can always use help drying."

Dale nodded to Miss Woodson, who sat rubbing her hands together with a smug look on her face. Looking away, he made his exit from the table. It didn't take him long to find Betsy on the side porch. She stood high on her toes, pulling clothespins from the sheets he'd hung the day before.

"Here, let me help you with those." As he reached over her shoulder to remove a clothespin, he caught a faint whiff of musky roses before she ducked out of the way. He knew the scent well due to Ma's love of Camay soap.

"I can do this without your help." She sure looked cute with her hands on her hips.

"True, but I feel like I owe you an apology for embarrassing you. I caused you to miss out on your last bite of pie." He pulled a pair of pins from a pillowcase.

"I think I had enough of the dessert and the conversation." She smoothed the pillowcase into a small rectangle and placed the item in a basket.

"Me, too. If it's any comfort, I really did tell my mother I'd follow up on some promises I made to her, before I start thinking about things involving where the supper conversation was headed." He felt a warm flush spread across his cheeks as her face took on a brighter hue.

"That's nice to hear. Tell me about your mother." Betsy picked up a lard bucket full of clothespins. She followed him as he released clips from the sheets and dropped them into the pail.

"Like you, she worked for Miss Woodson. She made meals for the family and lived in the kitchen, which was in the cellar of this house. I think Miss Woodson calls it the basement since she added on the upstairs kitchen. Fireplaces and woodstoves heated the rooms and provided a place to cook food back then. My mother still uses a wood burner back on the family farm. Once I get some savings built up, I plan to set her up with an electric or gas stove to make her life easier." He pulled one of the sheets from the line and held out one end.

She took the offered portion of the linen and they started the folding process. "Is buying her an appliance one of your promises?"

"No. If you asked her, she would rather use her old woodstove for cooking. I spent my first two years of life here in the cellar living with my mother. My birth pa was off fighting in the first war. She kept hoping he'd come whistling through the door. He didn't come back." They stepped closer for the final fold as he studied her hazel eyes, noticing both green and blue flecks. For a moment, she seemed to be studying him, too, until she chewed on her lip and looked down.

She turned away, grabbing a pillowcase to fold. "I'm sorry you lost your father."

"I never knew anyone but Papa Herbert. His cousin was my real pa. The family told him he needed to come and do right by my ma. So, he came and offered to marry her. She decided marrying would be a whole lot easier than trying to cook and keep a busy toddler away from the hot stove. Besides, Herbert's mannerisms reminded her of my real pa. They eventually grew to love each other and added my half-brother, Joseph, to the family. A few years ago, one of our widowed neighbors passed away, leaving an orphaned son. Ma and Papa Herbert took Gene in as another son during the last two years." Dale leaned against the porch railing as he reminisced.

Betsy laid the folded pillowcase in the nearby wicker basket. "I'm sorry you lost Joseph in the war. Did the orphaned boy have to serve?"

"No, he's younger. Thank the Lord. Gene stayed at home and did volunteer work in the community. Between serving the town and helping Papa Herbert keep up the farm, he stayed out of trouble, and still felt like he contributed to the war effort. He's entering his freshman year of college in the fall."

When she took down the other sheet, he reached out to help and brushed her hands, causing a shock of awareness. He chose not to acknowledge any reaction. After tucking the last of the linens into the basket, Dale lifted it into his arms. "Where would you like these taken?"

"We keep our extra linens in the pantry off the kitchen. Miss Woodson likes to call it her dragon's den. I'm not sure why, other than there is one plate with a dragon painted on it. The platter leans on a shelf for all to see. Maybe I should ask her about it one of these days."

Betsy's smile made Dale want to wrap his arms around the woman. It was good his hands held the laundry basket as he followed her through the door and into the house.

Chapter Eight

Betsy
1946

As brightly hued splashes of color painted the western sky, Betsy couldn't help but notice her feelings toward the man were changing. He had many admirable traits, for a friend. A friend would be enough for now. Some of the other women, like June, were ready to rush into a relationship. Betsy's experience with Ike Jones warned her to be wary.

The relationship had lasted long enough for the man to offer her a marriage proposal. Then he'd moved on to someone else at his next military assignment. She'd received a 'Dear John,' or should she say 'Dear Jane' note a month after his unit moved on to France. He'd held her heart while helping out at the powder plant. Rumors indicated he'd been a big flirt with others when they started moving in women like June and Margie to take over manufacturing duties.

Margie was the first one to hint at Ike's ways around the other girls. At first, Betsy assumed he only tried to be friendly, but then she'd watched several girls blowing kisses to him after he hugged her goodbye at the train station. She'd still held on to hope until she received his final note. He had promised her a life in the city. Instead, he only provided a big hole in her heart, which never healed enough to trust another man with more than friendship.

She made no plans to be deceived by a man's good looks again. She still hoped to find her way to the city one day. From the way Dale talked about being loyal to family, he'd surely head back to the farm when the powder plant closed its doors or changed to producing something not requiring a chemist.

She needed a distraction from her rambling thoughts. She walked over to her desk and pulled out the next poem from Missy. The title leapt from the page. Maybe the poem would reveal something about the pantry.

The Dragon's Den

Though fewer come to seek a place,
Where they can proudly bare their race.
The dragon's den still takes them in,
And hides their bodies, frail and thin.

When searchers come to seek their prey,
I choose my words, I don't betray.
There are two dens, one hidden well,
And where it is, I dare not tell.

The dragon breathes out his warm fire,
Protects his own within his byre.
And when it's time to send them out,
He opens doors without a shout.

The next crusader does his best,
To leave the dragon's den at rest.
No hints are left for those to find,
Who seek to steal from dragon kind.

This princess holds them all at bay,
They search but do not find a way,
To snare the runners from their goals,
Of finding freedom for their souls.

Betsy carefully held the poem to her chest and headed downstairs to see if Miss Woodson might be available to explain the mysterious words in the poetry. She found her employer sitting on the front porch glider. The older woman's soprano voice hummed "It is Well With My Soul." Betsy joined her on the swinging seat. Her alto voice provided harmony and echoes in the chorus. Together, they watched the sunset and pastel hues fade from the sky. A lone star began to twinkle in the darkening heavens.

Miss Woodson's deep sigh broke their silent contemplation. "The sky is beautiful tonight."

"I agree. God painted the sunset with my favorite colors." They gazed at the changing sky for a few moments more before Betsy broached the subject in the poem. "When I read one of your mother's poems tonight, I noticed she spoke of two dragon dens. Can you tell me if she gave you any details about the description? I know you've called the pantry a dragon's den when we've been working in there."

Miss Woodson chuckled. "Mother only told me a few stories about her involvement in the Underground Railroad. Fortunately, to answer part of your question, I do know why the pantry is the dragon's den. Early in her work with runaways, she told one of the local slave catchers about children visiting the house and christening the little room as the dragon's den. In one of her abolitionist poems, which my niece has, she mentioned a clue about hiding in a dragon's den, which was the nickname of their real hiding place. She and her aunts took the runaways to a hidden room, a dragon's den, somewhere in the cellar."

Betsy held up the poem and pointed to the reference of a second den. "It's a good thing none of those hunters ever found this poem. Have you ever seen the hidden room?"

"As a child, I was convinced there was a dragon living downstairs. I never ventured down the steps. So, I didn't look for a hidden room. I always assumed it was just a corner somewhere."

"This house is full of history. Would you mind if I nosed around a bit to see if I can spot the place?"

"You can try, but I doubt you will find anything. When we constructed the kitchen addition and switched over to a furnace, several years ago, the workers divided the basement differently. They never mentioned finding a hidden room and I didn't like walking down the steep stairs to check for myself."

"I may still take a closer look, if you don't mind." Betsy squirmed in her seat as curiosity poured into her soul.

"I don't have a problem with you looking around. In fact, you might ask Dale to go with you. He lived his first couple of years in the cellar, before we made the changes. I doubt he will remember anything from the time, but he seems intent on looking the place over. I assume he is searching for memories, but maybe there is more. We should write his mother and see if she remembers anything." Miss Woodson's raised eyebrows hinted she thought putting Betsy and Dale together in the basement was an excellent idea.

"I'll think about it." Betsy folded the poem, put it in her pocket, and wrapped her arms around herself as darkness fully covered the neighborhood. The air suddenly got chillier. Why was everyone pushing Dale into her business?

Ginny
Present day, January

Monday morning's snow-cleared roads meant school would be back to normal for Ginny's teaching day at Forest Glen Elementary School. Puddles of melted snow pooled on sun-drenched roads. Ginny and her students were heading back to their routines. She managed to keep down a breakfast of several plain crackers and a few sips of ginger ale, and only arrived a few minutes after the designated teacher arrival time. Her lessons from last Thursday and Friday would provide plenty for her students to work on for the next couple days. Her first chore would be sorting the stack of graded papers into her students' cardboard mailboxes.

"Hey, stranger, did you enjoy your snow days?" Melody stood in the doorway, surrounded by the twins.

Ginny paused and held back the information about being sick. "I managed to get quite a few boxes unpacked. Thanks to Scott and James being klutzy with my grandmother's old desk, we discovered a packet tying my grandparents to the Woodson House."

"That's pretty cool. So you are still friends with James?" A pink tinge crossed Melody's cheeks.

"Forgiveness is a healthy thing for both of us. What happened at college is in the past. He has changed into a better man." Her thoughts spun back to when Melody and James acted in roles for her musical. There might have been a spark then. "Are you interested in him?"

"No, I'm pretty busy right now with my buddies." She hugged the two children closer to her side.

"How was Chicago last week?" Ginny clapped her hand over her mouth. Maybe she shouldn't have asked in front of the twins.

"Busy. We can talk about it later." Melody nodded toward the children and barely shook her head. She waved goodbye and herded the twins from the room. "See you later, when you bring your class down for their lesson."

Ginny picked up the graded papers and sorted them into mailboxes for the students to retrieve later. Melissa and her foster parents would be proud of the child's high marks on the assignments. Since they'd all agreed to hold Melissa back, this was Ginny's second year with the child.

Her heart went out to the youngster who overcame abuse and neglect. Someday in the future, she hoped she and Scott could make a difference in a similar child's life through adoption. The work the Russell family did with foster children was amazing. However, Ginny wanted the more permanent adoption route. She prayed daily for Melissa and the Russell family, wondering how they dealt with not knowing when the courts might decide to send the girl home.

After sorting papers, she turned quickly toward the whiteboard to adjust the schedule written there. For a moment, dizziness threatened to make her tip over. She grabbed the side of her desk and forced air into her lungs. Moving slow would be a priority for the day. She sat down and laid her head on the desk for a moment.

"Are you okay?" Kara, her other close friend, leaned her head into the classroom. She stepped over and laid a hand on Ginny's back.

"I'm fine. I just needed a moment to get back into the swing of things. Those snow days spoiled me." Ginny faked a yawn and hoped it convinced her buddy all was well.

"I heard there were several kids with the flu. You better wash those hands today." Kara wrinkled her nose.

"Cleaning my hands is at the top of my list. So, how was your long weekend?" Ginny squirted a glob of hand sanitizer on her palms to underscore her attempt at cleanliness. She instantly regretted doing so as the sanitizer's chemical odor scented the air. She rose slowly and pulled open a nearby window, drawing in the fresh, cool breeze.

"Hey, don't freeze me out. Are you sure you're well?" Kara's shoes tapped across the floor. She laid a hand on her fellow teacher's forehead.

Ginny kept her face averted. She managed to reply in a calm voice. "I'm good. This sanitizer smells strong today." She tried to focus on something other than the odor. "It looks like someone made snow angels on the playground." Was her diversion too obvious? Kara was usually very perceptive.

The bell rang before her friend could say another word. Ginny turned with a forced smile, feeling a little green.

"I'll catch you later, maybe at lunch." Kara's expression let Ginny know she would get the third degree over the mid-day break, if she went. Her friend hustled away from the classroom door as the sound of stomping feet and chatter echoed from the hallway.

Pushing the window closed, Ginny stepped into the hall to watch the children line up boots in front of their lockers. When they finished, she greeted her students as they made their way to their desks. Seatwork, put out for last Thursday, sat on their table tops to keep them occupied until she started teaching in earnest. Melissa and her new best friend, Joy, shared a whispered conversation while they pulled their papers from the cubbies. The two classmates shared high-fives as they studied the positive comments on top of their respective papers.

Ginny managed to make it through the morning lessons. After a couple of hours, she lined up her students and dropped them off for music, making it a perfect day to get started back into the routine. By then her appetite returned and she devoured a peanut butter cracker snack pack while she set up a PowerPoint for her next lesson.

Afterwards, she walked down to the office to check her mailbox. "Hi, Denise, are you feeling better?"

"I am. Catching the latest virus is one of the hazards of working in a school. I'm sorry I missed your wedding. I hope you didn't spill any wedding cake or punch on Scott."

She laughed with the secretary as the woman teased her about marrying the man she'd run down in the hallway last spring. She'd dumped her half-eaten lunch on Scott when they first met. He'd come to recruit students for his summer drama camp. They had no idea at the time what lay ahead of them after their chance meeting.

"I was very careful to make sure everything turned out perfect. It was a beautiful event." Ginny pulled out her phone and shared proofs the photographer had sent. They spent several moments looking through the photos.

The woman leaned under her desk and pulled out a package. "Here's a little something from my family. I pray you two love birds have a happily ever after. I have a feeling you'll have a use for it once you get your wedding pictures printed." Denise handed her the belated wedding gift wrapped in white paper with a silver bow adorning the top. She urged the new bride to go ahead and open the gift.

Ginny peeled the wrapping paper from the box and found a filigreed silver picture frame. "It's beautiful and a lovely setting for a photograph of us at our wedding. Thank you, sweet lady." She held the gift close and headed toward the music room to pick up her students.

They did a quick turnaround by grabbing lunch boxes and heading back down the hall for their meal. Once they were in line, their teacher headed toward the lounge. She'd packed some of the leftover chicken soup in a microwavable container. As she waited for the food to warm, her phone pinged with a text from Scott. His acquaintance from work, Loretta Luterman, planned to rent Ginny's former home. Nice. The money would provide a bonus income when she took some time off to be with their baby. The scent of warm chicken broth emanated from the microwave and brought her mind back to lunch.

"Something smells good." Melody arrived with an enclosed container of her own. Ginny waved her friend to the microwave after removing her dish. Kara already claimed their customary spots at a table near a window. Her cell phone lay open on the table as she flipped through the contents using one hand, while taking bites of a sandwich with the other.

"Is there anything interesting in the news?" Ginny noted Kara's frown as the woman glared at her phone.

"It looks like there will be trouble if the levy doesn't pass in the May election. If the issue doesn't get the votes, there will be programs and teacher positions cut."

"I hope we get the vote then. Scott still hasn't received his official notice for tenure at the college. At this point we need both jobs, especially with..." Ginny's voice faded as she thought of her pregnancy and the papers they wanted to file for adopting.

"What did you say?" Kara's sharp gaze questioned her friend's dropped sentence.

Ginny swallowed back her concerns. "We just need to do our part by encouraging people to vote for the school levy. You know the three of us are the youngest teachers on the staff. If anyone is cut, it would probably be us."

Melody joined them with her hot plate of food. She took the empty seat next to Ginny. "What's going on? You two look like your best friend died. I know that can't be true because I'm the best buddy either of you ever had."

Kara shoved her phone across the table, so the aptly named music teacher could see the article.

"Oh my, it looks like art and music would be some of the first cuts." She laid her spoon across the top of her beef stew and shook her head.

The scent of warm beef gravy blended with savory chicken soup reached Ginny's nose, filling her with hunger and courage. She forced air into her lungs. Feeling stronger, she said, "We need to keep a positive attitude. This is a good community. The voters are usually supportive. I don't know about you, but I need to eat. Let's brainstorm about how we can help get the word out while we finish our food." She could not believe her stomach now took precedence over job concerns. Like a mama bear, she was ready to fight for her school's funding—after she devoured her lunch.

Chapter Nine

Dale
1946

Several weeks later, Dale pulled the waxed paper from the ham biscuit he'd managed to parse together from things found in the refrigerator and bread box. Miss Woodson mentioned boarders often took leftover food for their lunch. He'd taken advantage of the offer several times since moving in. He leaned against a tree outside the plant and savored each bite of the salty meat. It tasted better than the Spam provided by the army during his years on the Pacific front.

A group of his fellow workers ate around a picnic table. He should have joined them but two of the men held lit cigarettes and were freely blowing smoke into the faces of others. Tobacco was another thing the army provided the men. He'd sold his smoke ration to other soldiers and used the money to send gifts home to Ma and Papa Herbert.

He pushed away from the tree and walked in the opposite direction from the factory. The days were getting warmer and the lab was on the sunny side of the building. He'd take in as much of the breeze as he could before time to go back inside to work.

"Wait up, Dale." June's voice rang out across the lot. Several wolf whistles came from the table of fellow employees. Dale groaned. He knew better than to show rudeness, so he stuffed his fisted hands in his pockets and waited. She must have finished her morning shift and was heading home to Woodson House.

As they walked away from the factory, June grabbed his elbow and leaned in closer. He stiffened. She had no call to be so fresh with him, when he didn't show any interest. Dale unhooked her arm, stepped away, and faced the young woman.

"Look, June, you seem to be a nice person, but I'm really not interested. You need to accept my choice and look for someone else. There are plenty of other guys who would love to be your boyfriend. I don't have the time or interest."

June pouted. "I guess sweet Betsy already caught your eye. I'll be at the boarding house. If you ever change your mind, you know where to find me." She turned and walked away with her hips swaying. She looked over her shoulder and winked. The woman didn't give up easily. He shouldn't have been watching.

Turning back, he walked towards the factory, and into the lab. He thanked the Lord June didn't work in his department. The prayerful thought escaped involuntarily. Prayers hadn't come easy for a long time.

Dale lifted the box of explosives onto his lab table. The train brought a new shipment to the loading dock last night. His job was to take a small sample from each box and test it for efficacy. If it produced a certain color of flame and spark size, he'd send it on to the factory workers where they'd combine it with other materials for their blasting products. The factory provided major manufacturing for military explosives during the war. Now, they were experimenting with products for mining, emergency flares, and similar items. The market was much smaller for those goods, but for now it kept them in business.

Employees were well aware of potential layoffs. The boss told him his position might not last when they hired him. He just needed enough time to fulfill his mother's request.

For now, he shared the lab with his supervisor, Bob. The man used a cane due to a short tour of duty, early in the war. He'd come home after his injury and served his country by testing chemicals for the powder plant as a civilian. In addition to being a chemist, Dale's ability to lift the boxes proved to be an important asset to both men's duties.

Bob's cane thumped along the cement floor as Dale placed the tested box on a cart headed for the assembly line. "Sorry I'm late. I went to a meeting with the bigwigs over lunch. Things aren't looking too good for this old plant right now. We will have work through the summer, but afterwards, nothing is guaranteed."

"I understand." Dale lifted two boxes to the countertop.

The men worked alongside each other, testing the material in each container. Once they finished Dale loaded the completed boxes and pushed the cart onto the main floor of the plant. Bob stayed behind to tidy up the lab for their next experiments.

"Here you go, Allen. These are good to go." Dale parked the cart near one of the workstations.

"Thanks, man. Did Bob have any word from the top? I heard there was a meeting." Allen pushed his cap back and wiped sweat from his brow.

Dale enjoyed having conversations with the hardworking man. He reminded him of a younger version of his step-pa, Herbert. "We're good through the summer."

"Praise the Lord. Have you given any more thought to attending First Church with Verla and me on Sundays? There's several who attend from your boarding house."

"I know. The boarders have provided many invitations." Most of them from June, but Miss Woodson did her fair share of hinting about his ma expecting him to be in the Lord's House on Sunday. He'd felt a wave of guilt when Betsy raised her eyebrows and waited the first time he hadn't followed the group out the door on a Sunday morning for church. The last few weeks, she only shook her head. Her face displayed a sad expression when she followed the others down the street.

"Then you should come." Allen bent over and started placing boxes near his station on the assembly line.

"I'll get around to it eventually. I got out of the church habit during the war." Dale lifted a box. It only took a few moments to get everything off the cart.

"Then it's time to get back into the routine. If there's one thing my time overseas taught me, you're never promised another day. The Lord has helped me get through the big adjustment of coming home safe, when some of my friends didn't." He shook his head and closed his eyes as he sighed. It looked like he prayed, which made Dale want to squirm.

"I'll try to attend soon. You take care, Allen." Dale knew his friend was right. Ma dragged him to church the last time he visited home, previous to coming here to Forest Glen. He'd felt comfortable and bothered, all at the same time. Some heavy praying needed to be done before he'd feel God's hand in his life again.

While he'd escaped most wartime vices, he hadn't lived a life drawing anyone closer to God. He hid his faith under a mask of avoiding confrontations and going along with the crowd. Added to his hesitancy was a wash of guilt for not fighting on the front lines like his half-brother Joseph, who paid the ultimate price. Seeing his fellow chemist Bob leaning heavily on a cane served as a daily reminder about many soldiers who sacrificed more than a few years of uneventful duty.

As Dale pushed the empty cart toward the loading dock where train cars would bring in the next shipment of chemicals to investigate, a clatter of something falling and a curse came from the lab. He left the cart behind and rushed into the room. Bob sat on the floor. His cane lay nearby.

Bob's frustrated shouts pierced the air with anger. "I'm useless. I can't even walk across this stupid lab without tripping over my own cane. Too bad I didn't have some explosives to take me away from this misery."

Dale reached out to help. Bob pushed his hands aside and struggled to get up on his own, only to fall back to the floor. A commotion sounded from outside the lab as people came to check on the situation.

"Give us a minute, everyone. Bob just needs a little time." At least, Dale hoped his coworker would recover completely. He waved people back to work. Maybe he should rekindle his prayer life now, with a petition for the man groaning on the floor.

Please Lord, help Bob. Help me know what to say to him.

Ginny

Present day

Ginny rubbed her belly when a slight ache made her flinch. She hoped she hadn't injured the baby when she did a wild, sliding dance on a thin sheet of ice coating the sidewalks near the school. At least she hadn't hit the pavement. The ride home and climbing into the house provided discomfort, to say the least. Groans escaped from deep within as she leaned back into the study's loveseat. Maybe reading would distract her from the discomfort. She picked up another one of Missy's poems and began to peruse the verse.

Injured

My love came back missing half of one leg,
Refusing to talk, though I cry and I beg.
One leg at home and one lies in a grave,
Battered and torn, he refuses to shave.

Sam's days of fighting this war are all done.
But something is wrong with this town's favored son.
He does not seek comfort or help with the plight.
His shop is a prison; its doors locked up tight.

The voice that once called for this war to take place,
Sits silent, his head bowed in sorrow, disgrace.
I love him and hope for the day he will see,
His missing a leg doesn't change things for me.

Until he awakens from feeling this blow,
I know I must change; I'll take charge as I grow.
Once I was timid, relying on others,
Now I must speak for all sisters and brothers.

I must be strong so I'll take on the fight
Printing the news, sharing hope for what's right.
The women who've led in this battle are few.
This is our chance to show what we can do.

Our voice has been strong for both female and slave
We cannot give up; we must fight to the grave.
Our world is changing, we must stand our ground.
For votes and for freedom, let our words abound.

Ginny read the words penned by Missy from many years in the past.

Thoughts of supporting her educator position and those of the other young teachers entered her heart. She should rally her friends to stand up for their jobs. They needed a way to become involved in the campaign for the school levy vote and speak out to the community, something she wouldn't have dared to do, not so long ago. Maybe she could use her writing skills and newfound courage to compose an editorial for the local paper, still called *The Gazette*.

When she'd first started working on the musical for the historical museum, she'd been pretty timid. After going through the process of standing up for her creation, she'd become stronger. She'd learned to work with Scott and to forgive James. Forgiveness for his stealing an earlier musical work during college years proved to be a big step, but a good one. Composing and writing opened up her heart to a closer walk with God. People could change. It also helped her see there were good men, like Scott, in the world.

She held out her fingers as she studied her wedding and engagement rings. Satisfaction spread its wings and soared into her heart. Soon they would be a complete family with a child of their own. Maybe more than one child, if she ever got through the forms required by the adoption agency. Worry wormed its way across her shoulders. If she didn't have a job next year, would the reduction of income affect their chances of adoption?

She got up and walked to the window. This was not a time to go back to cowardly thoughts. Stretching her arms over her head, she lifted her voice and raised a song of praise. As inspired words and a tune rang out from her soul, the twinges of pain abated. God would take care of all her cares and doubts.

When all was lost, I looked above.
I saw the cross, bearing your love.
You took my doubt, filled up my heart.
Your gift of life, set me apart.

Forgiveness flowed, from your great gift.
And to that cross, my eyes still lift,
To see the Lamb, who took my sin,
And conquered death, my soul to win.

Forgive me Lord, when I'm not strong.
Please help me know, what's right or wrong.
May my life show, your presence here,
So all may see, what You hold dear.

"Your song was beautiful, honey." Scott stepped nearer and nuzzled the side of her neck. Ginny laughed as memories fluttered into her mind. Now she knew she was his honey. When she'd first gotten to know him, she thought he dated a girlfriend named Honey. It turned out Honey was a grandmother-aged friend in their church praise band. The woman was an amazing musician who would probably come up with a wonderful arrangement of the song she'd just sung.

"Is this a new song for church?" Scott turned her towards him and brushed a light kiss across her lips.

"It might be. Maybe Hope and I could sing it one Sunday for the downtown church. Then, Honey and the praise band could offer it as a special later on in the month at The Church of the Rock."

"The song sounds wonderful. When do you think it will be ready to go?"

"I'll have to put it on paper. It just came to me after thinking back on the last year and some of the things forgiveness helped me overcome. And having to ask forgiveness after being anxious about whether I will have a job next year." Ginny explained the situation at work as she sat down at the desk. She grabbed pencils and paper. Then she started putting the words down as she hummed through the piece again.

Scott helped her remember what she'd sung when she got stuck on one of the phrases. When they were finished, he leaned over her shoulder and wrapped his arms around her. "You are an amazing wife. God will be with us, no matter what the future brings. If you face a cut back, maybe you and Kara could share a job. Combining positions would allow more time for our children and still provide a position for the two of you."

"What an interesting thought, but it won't help Melody. She's got a family of her own to provide for since her brother and his wife are gone. She will need a full-time job to support the twins. I'm glad you're thinking of some ideas, though. We'll have to put you on our campaign committee."

"I'll see what I can do, but please don't put too much stress on yourself. You have our little one to think about." Scott's hovering shot a sense of over-protectiveness down her spine. She didn't like it.

"I'm good most of the day. I'll take care of my health." She leaned away from her husband and closer to the paper as she placed some punctuation marks between the words.

"Did you get an appointment with the doctor yet?" He was getting a little too pushy.

She had already made the call, but the need to have control of her life seemed to escalate from his questioning. "I talked to his office after school. There's an opening next Thursday at four. The opening was the first available time after school hours. I decided to take it." Ginny's voice rose as she moved away from Scott.

He raised his hands in the air and walked backwards, bumping into the side of the loveseat. His feet flipped into the air as he bounced over the armrest and onto the sofa cushions, before rolling to the floor. Both dogs promptly came over and started licking his face. Tension dropped from her shoulders as she and Scott burst into laughter over his predicament.

"Sorry, my emotions are riding a roller coaster today." She reached out a hand, which Scott took.

When she tried to pull him up, he kissed her palm. Then he used his own strength to climb onto the couch without assistance. "Please let me know if I push you too hard. We're a team, but I can give you room to breathe if you need some space."

She plopped down beside him. "Thank you. I think I do need a distraction right now. Maybe a chapter from my grandmother's manuscript would be just what the doctor ordered."

Chapter Ten

Betsy
1949

Betsy poured over another chapter of *Lo, Michael*. Miss Woodson and most of the other boarders had left after dinner to attend a new movie together. Betsy chose reading in solitude. The rumbling of the evening train, bringing freight for the powder plant, provided the only interrupting sound so far. She turned her focus back on the book after hearing the train thunder through town.

The novel provided a welcome distraction from all the events occurring during the last few weeks at the boarding house. Michael, in Grace Livingston Hill's book, portrayed the perfect golden-haired man: angelic, strong, handsome, humble, and willing to fight for the underprivileged. He was nothing like her betrayer Ike, or the dark-haired man everyone except June seemed to push her toward. When the rich looked down on Hill's character, Michael, he looked up to the sky and took on another challenge for the poor. He reminded her of a superman, like the one in comic books she'd seen at the newspaper stand downtown.

Though she'd read the tome several times, the purchase of a farm to solve his friend's poverty didn't set right with her as she read through the account this time. She'd paid her dues on the family farm and knew the lifestyle provided food, but definitely not riches. Though, a simple farm life was all Michael wanted for the families. She propped up her chin with her hand and looked outside at the fading daylight. Michael's farm would provide something to meet their basic needs so they didn't choose a criminal path.

Her goals of finding her way to the city for stability and independence clashed with the theme of Hill's book. The words seemed to preach a sermon against all her latest plans. She put the novel aside and reached for the next poem in the stack.

The poem mentioned the love of Missy's life coming home from the war with the loss of a leg. He was another idealistic male brought low by the realities of life. Missy was right not to wait on the man to heal. Her poetry indicated she would stand on her own and continue to work for *The Gazette*. Brave women like her proved they were the backbone of the world when true heroes didn't exist.

Margie demonstrated she could adapt after her job status changed to part-time. She hadn't become a Fullerette for the brush company. Selling didn't fit her personality. Instead, she'd found a position at the local library, completely replacing her factory hours. The wages weren't quite as high, so she still helped with evening meals for the boarders. A pleasant expression replaced the one she'd worn since learning the fate of her job at the plant.

June still tried to catch Dale's attention, but she had the sense to try different tactics lately. Every evening meal now boasted sweet desserts served with an even sweeter smile from the young woman, who looked demurely at the floor as she passed out the delicacies she'd made during her open afternoons. Dale managed to avoid her as much as possible.

Several times Betsy found him pacing around the basement, looking puzzled. She'd asked if he needed something but he shook his head, saying he doubted anyone could help. She'd been tempted to ask if he knew anything about the dragon's den but decided to avoid getting further involved.

The sound of a thump, coming from the heating vents, made her jump. What in the world? The furnace hadn't been running for several weeks now. Breezes blew through open windows, whisking lacy curtains into her room as the sun dipped below the horizon. She slipped back into her shoes and trekked down the stairs.

One time last summer, she'd removed a trapped squirrel from the chimney pipe. She'd been able to deal with the animal after being a farm girl all her life. She sighed. Perhaps there were a few benefits of having a country background. Though, having someone braver and stronger at hand would be a positive thing for a change.

When she opened the basement door, the lights were already on. Strange, she usually turned them off. The thump sounded again, making the hair stand up on her arms despite the warmth of early summer.

"Is anyone down here?" Her voice sounded shaky. She took in a deep breath of musty air and forced confidence into her chest as another thump sounded from the furnace room. "I said, is anyone here?"

The noise stopped. Dale peered around the doorframe. "I'm sorry. I thought everyone went to the movies."

Betsy put her hands on her hips. "So you decided to attack the furnace while we were all out?"

"No, I thought it might be the right time to look for an item my mother left here." The man looked guilty of something. She wasn't sure of what.

"Miss Woodson said this furnace wasn't even around when you lived here." She stepped closer to see if he'd done any damage.

"It wasn't, but the pipe for the woodstove Ma used may be the same one the furnace uses." He ran his hands around the stovepipe's entrance to the wall and tapped the wall with the hammer in his hand.

"Do you think your mother put something in the pipe?" Her curiosity rose as she wondered what he hoped to find.

"No. There may have been a place near the pipe where she hid an item meaning a great deal to her."

"Then why didn't she take it with her?" Something Miss Woodson had said about a secret room or dragon's den filtered into her thoughts. They'd written Dale's mother a note, but hadn't received an answer yet. She wondered if Dale looked for the same space.

"Ma wasn't thinking clearly when she left here. She'd been sick and found it troublesome keeping up with the demands of a full household. My step-pa shook her off balance when he offered her a better chance at life, for both of us. Apparently, he'd come into town on a mission of bringing her back into the family one way or another."

Dale stopped his tapping and turned, meeting Betsy's gaze. "He was the last of the Nash line alive after the first war ended, other than me. The woman Papa Herbert thought he loved jilted him, so he gave up on marriage until his family forced his hand. My grandparents were getting older and wanted the farm to go to one of their descendants. My pa's cousin figured a marriage of convenience would answer their prayers by having me be a part of their declining years."

"It took a big leap of faith for both of them." Betsy hardened her heart against the romantic idea of having such a trusting kind of faith. Dale's family would definitely expect him to move back to the country for his inheritance. The knowledge about his family took him out of her consideration for sure, not that she was interested. He'd be better off with June, who hoped for a marriage to anyone.

Dale crossed his arms and leaned against the basement wall. "I'm not sure if it was faith or desperation. Regardless, when he made the offer to take care of us through the name only marriage, Ma turned in her resignation here, and stuffed the few things we owned into the trunk of Herbert's Model T. One of my first vague memories is hearing his car's loud noise and clinging to Ma, as Miss Woodson waved good-bye."

"Did your mother ever mention a dragon's den?"

"Only in fairy tales, why do you ask?" He stepped closer to the light bulb illuminating the space. The waves in his dark hair gleamed under the light.

Betsy swallowed before she could answer. "The other day, Miss Woodson mentioned her mother hinting about a secret room somewhere in the basement. She never knew the exact location, but said it was used for the Underground Railroad."

"You mean slaves were hidden in this house before the Civil War?" His eyes beamed with curiosity.

"She heard about the information through family lore. We thought maybe you or your mother might remember something about a hidden room." The sparkle in his eyes sent a ripple across her chest as she waited for his answer.

"I don't have any recollection of the place, but I do wonder if the room might be where Ma hid her treasure." He turned back to the wall and laid a hand against it. His gaze searched the gray surface.

"What is your mother's treasure?" The thrill of searching for something coursed through Betsy's bones.

"Ma wouldn't tell me. She didn't want me to be disappointed if I didn't find it. I was to keep my search a secret unless I found something." His eyes looked troubled.

"I won't give away her secret." Betsy watched as his shoulders lowered and his face relaxed into a smile, after she gave her promise. "Did she give you any hints?"

"The only clue she gave was she'd hidden a family heirloom in the space, stored in a Whitman's Chocolate sampler box."

"Yum, I love their candies. I like the chocolate-covered fruit creams the best. They're a treasure all on their own." Betsy placed a hand over her waist and knew she smiled at the thought of the rich candies.

"I favor the nut ones myself." He tapped a few more times before lowering his hammer and shoulders. "I'm not hearing any hollow spaces. Maybe it's nuts to even try looking, but I made Ma a promise. I don't think we're going to find anything unless we have permission to tear into this wall." He walked toward the exit from the furnace room.

"Why do you think the wall you were touching is where it might be?" Betsy followed his broad back.

"Ma mentioned something about it being near a fireplace or oven. As near as I can tell, that stovepipe connects to one of the original chimneys in this house. It would make sense for the hidden place to be nearby. If there was a secret room, it doesn't look like it is here anymore." A frustrated growl provided evidence of his disappointment.

"Maybe your memory isn't serving you correctly. Don't give up hope until we've gotten a letter back from your mother. You could try calling her." Betsy touched his wrist to comfort him, and then quickly pulled her hand away as a shock of awareness blitzed down her arm.

His eyes widened briefly, then he looked away. "A letter would be best. Ma doesn't like talking on the phone and some of our party line folks are pretty nosy. She wanted to keep this a secret. She seemed pretty embarrassed about leaving the hidden item behind. I probably shouldn't have even told you about my search. I just felt I could trust you and it kind of spilled out."

"You don't have to worry about me telling anyone. You might want to confide in Miss Woodson. We talked about the dragon den not too long ago. Her memory can be spotty at times, but she seems to remember quite a bit about her mother's adventures helping people escaping slavery."

Ginny
Present day, February

Students gathered around Ginny and the volunteer docent standing in front of the Woodson House's hidden room. Melissa raised her hand and the woman nodded to the young girl.

Melissa posed her question with a swagger that wouldn't have been there a year ago. "Is this the place we called the dragon's den when we did the musical last year?"

The volunteer looked confused, so Ginny answered. "You're right, Melissa. When I researched this Underground Railroad station, I discovered the people who lived here many years ago did refer to this hidden room as a dragon's den." She shared a smile with her sweet student.

The older woman chuckled. "I'm afraid I missed the show due to the birth of a grandchild. I heard it was a good production."

"It was. I got to be in the play." Melissa bent at the waist and executed a small curtsy.

The docent smiled. "You are brave to be on stage. I'd be too scared to stand in front of a big crowd."

"The play had some scary parts. I'm glad I didn't live when slavery was around." Melissa shuddered before she smiled at Ginny. "My teacher helped me be strong."

Ginny acknowledged the girl's compliment with a nod as she struggled to keep the tears from flowing. Crying was the last thing she needed to do in front of her students. Her emotions overflowed at the least little heart pull lately, a side effect of pregnancy, according to the internet.

She pointed to the small room exposed for viewing behind a Plexiglas shield and attempted to focus her students' attention on the tiny space. "What do you think it would have been like to travel up from the ravine and then hide quietly in this secret room?"

"It would have been hard for me to stay still in a small space," one of the boys piped up.

"I think being safe and scared at the same time would make me be quiet," another student replied as she crossed her arms and shivered.

After several students answered the question, Ginny turned and indicated the docent should continue the tour.

"Next to the hidden room, you will see there's a fireplace which served as the Woodson family's oven. Today we cook our roasts and cookies using a gas or electric stove. Back then, people heated their food with wood in a metal or brick oven. As a child, one of your chores might have been gathering wood for the fireplace."

Several students grumbled about chores until Ginny cleared her throat and gave them a 'teacher look,' bringing their attention back to the tour guide.

"This fireplace also kept the runaways warm and hidden when slave catchers hunted for them. Even this far north in Ohio, there was a group of people who didn't support freedom for the enslaved people." The docent continued to talk about some of the smaller items on display in the room before giving the students a few moments for asking questions.

After further exploration of the room, the woman directed the class to another part of the basement. The next room provided informative displays about the Underground Railroad and the restoration of the old house.

Melissa edged near Ginny and whispered, "This is where it really happened, isn't it?"

"Yes." The awe on the child's face sent a thrill into her teacher's chest. Goosebumps rose on her arms. "It sure is, sweetheart. This old house inspired the musical, *Incident at Woodson House*. I'm so glad you were able to be in the production." The play had given the child self-confidence and a realization of her value as a person.

A yearning to be Melissa's mother surged into her heart. She knew the possibility of adopting the child would never happen. The girl lived in a good home with the Russell family. She might also have a satisfactory placement with her own mother, if the woman ever proved herself worthy of being a parent.

Praying for the situation was the only thing Ginny could do at this point. Prayers for Melissa, prayers for those parenting the child, and prayers Ginny and Scott might one day find love for a child who needed them as much as Melissa needed the Russell family. A rumble in her stomach reminded her she had someone else to pray for, a small unborn child produced by the love for her husband.

Ginny clapped her hands to get the students' attention long enough to thank the docent and line up for the next stop on their field trip. They headed toward the historical museum where the curator, Annie, would be presenting the local history of early settlers in a reclaimed cabin donated by a family from a nearby community. They passed another fourth-grade class, led by Kara, on the sidewalk as they exchanged sites. Annie greeted Ginny from the door of the log home with a wave. Students from both classes did their own greetings by chatting and fist bumping.

Melissa shouted to one of her friends in the other class, who had also played a role in the musical. "You get to see the dragon's den in the Woodson House. It's the real one instead of the fake one in the play."

Both lines of children grew animated as their talk escalated about a rumored dragon living in the basement. Ginny halted both lines and gave a brief explanation before speculation got out of hand. Once everyone settled back into their lines with a better understanding of history, the teachers led their classes to their next destinations.

Annie ushered Ginny's class into the log structure. The students took their places on small benches provided by the museum. The curator talked about early pioneer cooking, chores, and culture. When she finished her speech, she asked for questions from the students.

"Are there any hidden rooms in this cabin?" One of the boys squirmed in his seat.

"I don't know of any, unless you consider the attic a hidden space. The parents were the only ones with a bed here on the main floor. Once the children were old enough, they climbed up a ladder and slept on a straw mattress lying on the attic floor." Annie smiled and pointed to another student with a raised hand.

"I wonder if they ever called it a dragon's attic."

"I guess they could have. Children needed to use their imagination back then since there were few toys and lots of work helping their parents on the farm."

"Maybe we should write a poem about a dragon's den of your choosing when we get back to school." The students received their teacher's idea with both excitement and moans. Their cries covered Ginny's whimper from a short-lived abdominal ache.

Chapter Eleven

Betsy
1946

Excitement bubbled inside Betsy when she unfolded the next poem in the packet. The title mentioned the dragon's den. This might be the perfect excuse to pick through both Miss Woodson and Dale's thoughts about the title given to Woodson House's special secret. Surely the hidden room Dale searched for and the place where the runaways hid were the same. She ran her finger down the faded page, savoring the words and hoping for some clue.

Dragon's Den Dilemma

Running footsteps splash and flurry,
Flee from hunters, in a hurry.
Seek my castle's guiding light,
Where I'll hide them, out of sight.

Waiting in the dragon's lair,
They may sleep without a care,
Knowing that he guards them well,
Warming in his freedom cell.

In another place in town,
Dragon Sam sits with a frown.
Holding anger from the past,
Hoping each day is his last.

Once he helped friends find my den,
Now he will not let us in.
I pray for changes in his heart,
May his sadness soon depart.

The dragon's den is full tonight,
Sam's help is needed in this fight.
He has the space to house two men
But his door's closed, they can't come in.

Betsy shut her bedroom door as she headed down the stairs. It was sad the poem turned to a reflection of a bad time in Sam Woodson's life, but his depression wasn't the important thing she'd thought of when she studied the poem. Missy mentioned warmth in the dragon's den. Dale talked about a room near an old fireplace oven. The places must be the same. If only they could locate the hideaway.

The sound of voices drew her to the front room. Several of the boarders sat around a card table playing a game of Rook. Dale and Miss Woodson chatted in one corner of the room. A blue scarf emerged from her employer's knitting needles and hung down the side of her padded rocker. The sound of his laughter tickled her ears. Perfect.

Betsy pulled a stool near them and held out the brittle paper. "Look at this poem from Miss Woodson's mother. I think Dale's hidden room and the second dragon's den must be the same space. They were both warm places down in the cellar."

Dale took the offered paper and scanned the poem. "You might be right. There's more to the poem than the hiding place. Too many men came home from war then, and now, with problems that make everyday living hard."

Miss Woodson laid down her knitting and stared into the distance. "My father had a great deal of trouble accepting what happened to him during his service in the Civil War. The loss of his foot was only a small part of the battle he fought in his mind for the rest of his life. It took him a while to forgive himself and those who caused the war. His injury did go deeper than the amputation, but Mom didn't give up on him. She encouraged him to be open about what happened, to talk, and write about the changes and events."

Dale nodded but seemed lost in thought as Miss Woodson gazed at his face.

Betsy squirmed at the silence between the two. How had the conversation gotten off track? "I wish your mother talked more about the dragon's den. The information would have helped us find the hidden room." Betsy reached for the paper and studied the words again. "I wonder what she did with the extra men who needed a place to stay the night."

Miss Woodson chuckled. "I'm sure she found help. Traditions suggest there were several Underground Railroad stations in Forest Glen. There's a house a couple of blocks away that may have used their attic as a hiding place. It belonged to my brother, Warren, at one time. On the road leading north out of town there's a barn with a high loft. Some say runaways hid there too. However, times were desperate and people on the run had no problem crowding into whatever space my mother provided for them to hide in."

Ginny
Present day, February

Ginny squeezed close against Scott. There was standing room only in the crowed space. It didn't look like another person could possibly edge into the board meeting. Her two fellow schoolteachers, Melody and Kara, pressed next to them, shoulder to shoulder. The people around them murmured in concern as the board president read off the list of possible cuts.

"If the levy fails, we will be upping the class sizes to the maximum number allowed by the state. If we go over the limited population it will be more economical to hire classroom aides at lower wages, than to hire another teacher. This will allow us to cut one teacher from each of the elementary grades. We'll be dropping art and music for the lower level. Reductions to part-time will take place for physical education. If the state didn't require P.E., we would cut the class completely. If a high school class has less than twenty students enrolled, the class won't be offered. Sports will become pay-to-play. Busing will be eliminated for those closer than two miles from their buildings."

Several in the crowd raised a negative cry.

"My daughter loves the arts. Those classes are the only place she feels comfortable." Tears formed in one woman's eyes.

"What about the purposely small gifted and advanced placement classes? I chose to live in town because of those opportunities for my children." One of Scott's fellow professors frowned at the chairman of the school board.

One man raised a fist. "My son is this coming year's star quarterback. We can't afford to pay for our heating bill this month, much less his sports."

As more voices called out questions, the board president rapped with his gavel and called for order. "Then we all need to vote for this levy. If you have the time to campaign, we have a committee willing to find a place for you to work." After announcing a few details about after school activity cuts, the meeting adjourned.

Ginny's heart beat faster as people grumbled about paying more in taxes. Some expressed disbelief about whether the cuts would even be made. She knew better. The board recently denied requests for field trips for the rest of the year. At least she'd gotten the trip to the historical museum in before the edict took effect. She'd purchased her own paper to run off worksheets for the last few weeks. The teachers' union sent out an updated seniority list a few days ago. Ginny and her friends were at the bottom of the list. Melody clasped her hand. Kara held onto their shoulders.

"We can do this. We'll work together to save our jobs. Our great-great-grandmothers got us the vote. Surely we can get this vote passed." Kara squeezed them together into a tight trio. They'd made it through college as friends. Working in the same school system brought them even closer during the last few years.

"I'll do what I can to help." Scott's supporting voice bolstered Ginny's morale.

Even though the board meeting ended, the group of friends and many other teachers surged forward to pick up leaflets placed on the front of the stage. Each stack had neighborhood street names attached with suggested conversation starters. Volunteer information suggested not dropping the pamphlets on doorsteps. It would take the human connection to make a difference. Personal conversations with others would help the cause. This type of contact wouldn't be easy. Earlier, many unsettling comments echoed around the room from those gathering to fight against higher taxes, but they needed to try. Ginny found the packet marked for their neighborhood and signed the list, pledging her support.

Scott picked up a handful of papers without a street assigned. "I'll see if I can share these with some of my co-workers."

Dale
1946

Dale sorted through the stack of papers, checking to make sure his figures were correct. He enjoyed working with chemicals and observing reactions. Recording information onto the paperwork as part of his position held less appeal than his experiments. More paperwork rattled nearby as Bob leaned over his own stack, muttering about a problem. Dale decided not to bother asking what the matter was. The man could find something to grumble about in any situation.

He reckoned the dislike of completing the forms was one area they could agree on. He paperclipped his work together and placed it in the appropriate file cabinet drawer before starting his final cleanup for the day. When he turned away from his clean tabletop, he noticed Bob's slumped shoulders. He couldn't leave without at least saying goodbye.

"Hey, Bob, you have a good evening."

"I would if I could." The man swung off his chair and thumped to the file cabinet, using the wall as a support. Stuffing his work into the drawer, he returned for his cane and headed for the office door.

"Do you need some help with anything?" Dale held the door open.

Bob answered Dale's question with a glare and a shake of his head. "You wouldn't understand."

"Give me a try. I'll never know what you need unless you want to share." Dale clicked the door closed behind them and used his key to lock the office.

The man harrumphed as they walked outside. "I've got a family to support. Being a chemist wasn't my first choice of careers. My parents made the decision for me. They said being an artist would never pay. They were right, of course."

Dale masked his surprise, fighting against saying something offensive to the man. "Do you ever take the time to create any art?"

"Not too often, though I did do some paintings to decorate my little boy's bedroom. My wife seemed to like my attempts to depict nursery rhyme scenes." Bob's lips curled into a half smile then flattened. "Painting won't pay the bills once this job is gone."

"Have you thought about the Serviceman's Readjustment Act?"

Bob scratched his head. "You mean the G.I. Bill?"

"Yeah, that's what I'm talking about. Maybe you could go back to college and study something related to art. During my service in the military, there were people who drew pictures of the tires and the vehicles they were placed on. I think they called themselves draftsmen or commercial artists."

"The draft is what got us all into the war. I'm not so sure about becoming a draft man." He chuckled. "The commercial art might be interesting but I'm not sure if I'm good enough for those kinds of details. I like to dabble in all kinds of art. I've done some wood sculpting. You might call it whittling."

Dale could not believe Bob's rare show of humor. "Maybe you could be an art instructor at a school. Then you could use all kinds of art supplies. You might have to sharpen up your people skills."

"I was quite a friendly guy at one point." He stopped walking and pointed his cane at Dale. "After taking a hit during the war, my outlook changed for the worse. Sorry. Maybe I should think about a career change."

"You could always use your chemistry degree to invent a new type of paint." Dale imagined his acquaintance in a lab coat, bent over a barrel of exploding paint. He chuckled as his mind pictured a canvas with a burst of splatters all over it. Who would want a piece looking like the floor in a paint factory?

"Interesting, but I might warm up to the idea of being a teacher. My wife took care of a whole group of little ones while the other women worked at the factories. I enjoyed helping the kiddies do some art projects at our house." A thoughtful expression appeared on Bob's face. Dale had never seen him so relaxed.

"Then I vote for you to explore becoming a teacher. You'd be able to choose between teaching art and science." Dale stopped in front of Woodson House and clapped his co-worker on the back before bidding him goodbye.

"I guess the ballot has been cast." Bob hobbled down the street using a quick pace.

Dale held back a chuckle. Most days the man barely forced one foot in front of the other.

Chapter Twelve

Ginny
Present day, late February

Ginny forced her tired feet to move up the stairs to the next doorway. When someone answered her knock, she began her practiced appeal. "Please consider voting for the schools in the upcoming election. The students need your support." Ginny attempted a smile. Her face muscles stiffened from trying to appear pleasant all evening.

The frowning woman in front of her stared at the pamphlet. "I raised my kids a long time ago. Now my income is fixed and I can't afford another tax draining my accounts. My husband and I have made lots of cuts in our living style. The school system needs to budget their money better."

The woman slammed the door shut before Ginny could get another word out of her mouth. A fleeting twinge crossed her belly. Her feet ached from hours of walking. Darkness made the evening chill colder. Thoughts of calling it a day flittered though her mind, but she wasn't a quitter. If she went to the next house, she'd fulfill her promise to spread her allotted number of flyers for the day.

Putting one foot in front of the other, she trudged down the sidewalk to the last home on her list. Praying for a positive response, she rang the doorbell and waited. A senior-aged woman with short-cropped hair and wire-rimmed glasses smiled at her through the storm door. She decided to try a more personal appeal.

"Hi, my name is Ginny Cline-Hallmark. I'm a fourth-grade teacher at the elementary school and would appreciate your vote for the schools in May." She held out the paper.

The woman wrapped her hand around Ginny's and drew her into a small foyer. "I know you from the play last year. You wrote the musical and took the lead on the final night. My husband and I loved the performance. Please come in out of the cold and tell me about the school's needs."

Weight fell from Ginny's shoulders as the woman welcomed her into a small sitting room. An open newspaper revealed the letter to the editor Ginny submitted to the paper a few weeks ago. Due to time constraints, she hadn't taken time to see it in print. A quiet gentleman nodded from his easy chair, his focus on a game show.

"We don't get out much these days, so I'm happy to have someone to chat with besides my online friends. My sweetheart has been declining lately." She smiled at the man and he gave a slight wave to Ginny. "Can I get you something warm to drink?" The white-haired woman rubbed her hands together.

Ginny shook her head as she sat down. Relief poured over her tired body. "Thank you, but I'm good. The information about the school levy is on this flyer and in the newspaper you have right here. If we don't get the vote, many student opportunities face cuts. More children will be in each classroom with fewer teachers."

The woman patted her arm. "I was a teacher in my younger years. I understand where you are coming from. Would you mind if I shared the information on my podcast, *Annabelle's Answers*? I've been studying what you wrote in *The Gazette*. Maybe my words will influence the voters."

Ginny's mouth fell open. She swallowed. When she met the woman moments ago, she never would have guessed the lady knew any technology skills or understood how to be a podcaster. "Getting the news out through online media would be wonderful. Please let me know if you need anything."

"I'll tell you what, why don't you line up a few of your teacher friends and come back here on Saturday afternoon at two o'clock? We'll do a recording and get the word out to the community about the school situation. Do you like the idea of doing a promotional podcast?"

Ginny barely knew the woman but couldn't resist hugging her. "This is the best news I've received all day."

~~~~~

The following Saturday, Ginny, Kara, and Melody sat on one side of Annabelle's kitchen table. They faced an oversized microphone and Annabelle's grown grandson, who Kara watched with an ear-to-ear grin. Ginny gave her friend an elbow poke and mouthed "pay attention."

Kara whispered back, "I am," as she smiled at the blond-haired man focusing on his laptop.

"Grandma, can you ask the question again? I'm going to have to do some editing of the last few minutes." He shook his head at the younger women and nodded to Annabelle.

"As I was saying, I'd like to hear how this school levy will affect each of these teachers. Melody is a music teacher. What a lovely name. It suits your career choice."

Melody leaned closer to the microphone. "Thank you, Annabelle, for allowing me to share. Music and art are important parts of children's education. There are many children who find their safe place in the arts. Besides being creative outlets, both subjects provide creative ways to discover information about cultures and history."

"But what if the levy fails?" Annabelle raised her eyebrows and
~~~~~

waved for Melody to continue.

"Art and music instruction would be either eliminated or cut drastically." Her voice shook. Then she straightened. "I'm a single mother, who would be in search of a new position. My brother's surviving children, whom I adopted after his recent tragic death, would no longer have a home here. I hoped this would be a new beginning for them."

"Being forced to move those children again would be a loss for your whole family and the community." Annabelle laid a hand on Melody's arm. "What about you other ladies? I understand you are both fourth-grade teachers. Surely those jobs should put you in more secure positions." She pointed to Ginny.

"It should be, but as I mentioned to you a few days ago, one of the planned cutbacks is to put more children in each classroom. The result would be layoffs. Both of us are newer than other teachers in the district. We would be the first to go."

Kara leaned in closer to the microphone. "Our school system is one of the best in the area. We would like to see the district continue to thrive. A positive vote will help us provide your children with what they need to succeed."

After several more comments, Annabelle wound up the conversation. "Well said, teachers. Thank you, Melody, Kara, and Ginny, for sharing your perspective as teachers."

"Thank you for having us today." Ginny squeezed the older woman's hand. Kara and Melody nodded.

"I appreciate all you do as teachers serving the children of this town, ladies." She returned Ginny's squeeze with a firm grip and kept talking. "I know many of my senior friends are concerned about the extra tax money, but I've seen the figures. This levy for the school system isn't going to overburden most of us. When we look at how an effective education makes our town appealing to those searching for a great place to live, it makes me want to be a supportive voter. Thank you for listening. This is Annabelle signing off with answers for another week." She gave her grandson a nod. He tapped a few keys on his laptop. Everyone else leaned back in their chairs, giving a collective sigh of relief.

Exhaustion overwhelmed Ginny's limbs as she collapsed into one of Annabelle's kitchen chairs. For a moment, the world tilted as black spots swam along the sides of her vision. She'd never fainted before but remembered to lean forward. Forcing her focus to the floor, she pretended to inspect her shoelaces until her head stopped spinning.

"Are you all right, dear?" Annabelle's voice infiltrated her swirling mind.

Ginny lifted her head up and sucked a deep breath into her lungs. "I'm fine now. I just needed to..."

The older woman laid her arm around Ginny's shoulder. "I think I understand." Her smile said she did grasp the situation.

Laying a finger on her lips, Ginny looked at her fellow teachers, who were busy chatting with the woman's grandson.

A knowing grin crossed Annabelle's face and she nodded her head. "Don't worry, child. Your secret is safe with me."

~~~~~

A few days later, Ginny noticed Mom's number appearing on her phone's caller ID. She debated answering. Keeping secrets from her mother was almost impossible. However, not answering would only bring more questions. She sighed and made the connection. "Hi, Mom."

"Hi, sweetheart, I am thinking of having the family over for lunch after church tomorrow. Would you and Scott be able to join us? Your brother said he could come, and you know Nathan."

Her mother's voice sounded bubblier than usual. She put the phone on speaker. "Coming over sounds great. I'm pretty sure we don't have any plans tomorrow afternoon. Are you free to visit Mom and Roy, Hon?" She looked at her husband sitting at his desk.

He nodded. "I always enjoy visiting your mom."

Ginny's curiosity pulled at her like a tug-of-war rope. "So, Mom, you sound excited. Did you get another contract for illustrating a book?"

Mom giggled. A man's voice echoed in the background. "No, nothing involving a book release. Roy will be here. He's planning on bringing in a carryout meal for everyone."

"Nice." Ginny fought the urge to laugh as she said her goodbyes. Maybe they'd finally settled on a date for their wedding. He'd asked for Ginny's blessing when he walked her down the aisle as Scott's bride. Mom's engagement ring was stunning. There was no need to delay a wedding date since they were not getting any younger.

Scott's eyebrows rose. "Dinner sounds nice, but are you going to be able to keep your morning sickness in check?"

"I do okay after mid-morning. I should be able to handle a meal with the family." At least she hoped so. She'd mostly coped during school days by eating lots of crackers and lemon candy. She'd even managed to eat a few things at the church dinner a few weeks ago.

"Maybe we should bring a mild side dish your tummy can handle." Scott closed his computer and leaned back in his chair.

Ginny pecked his cheek. His bristled skin rasped against her lips. "I knew there was a reason I married you. I'll go figure out something to cook." She headed off to look through her grandmother's cookbook. Jezebel scurried along behind her. Over the years, her hound learned the word 'cook' meant food. Her built in floor sweeping dog would take care of any falling crumbs. Carlos trailed behind. The chihuahua was a quick
~~~~~

learner.

Ginny pulled the old book from her shelf and flipped through the pages. As she neared the back, she perused the handwritten recipes at the rear of the book. Most of the notes were in her grandmother's curling script. One of the notes displayed a different penmanship. 'From your mother, Betsy Nash,' headed a recipe for lemon tarts.

"Scott, come and see what I found!" She jumped up from the kitchen table and they met in the hallway. He grabbed her around the waist. The book pressed against both of them. Ginny squealed in delight.

"Is something wrong, honey?" Scott held her at arm's length. His gaze went to her belly.

She looked into his concerned eyes. "I'm fine. There's a lemon tart recipe in Grandma Stuart's cookbook written in Great-grandmother Betsy's handwriting."

Scott's shoulders relaxed. A smile like a ray of sunshine spread across his face. "Lemon tarts sound like the perfect dessert for my sweet wife and mother of our child. Maybe we should tell your mother."

Panic piled up in Ginny's mind. "No, like I said, she wasn't really encouraging about us wanting to have a child so soon."

Scott chuckled. "I meant about us bringing dessert. We don't want to upstage your mother if she has other plans."

"I think our dessert will be a surprise. No one can turn down the extra sweetness." She pulled two aprons from a hook near the kitchen door. She wrapped one of them around Scott's waist and laughed at his expression. Sunflowers must not be his style. Too bad. He needed a cooking lesson from Great-grandmother Betsy.

Betsy
1946

Betsy worked the lard into the flour. She knew a few things about making a pie crust. Even if cooking wasn't her favorite chore, her mother had taught her how to make several types of pastries and pies. Miss Woodson asked Betsy to see if there were any lemons at the market. There had been a fresh bag, enough for lemonade and tarts for supper. Margie's job at the library recently became full-time, so Betsy once again helped with some of the meal preparation. June planned on frying pork chops for dinner. The blonde had given up on catching Dale's attention with desserts. Betsy's tarts would be the first sugary treat in several weeks. Fresh green beans and creamed corn would supplement the main entree for June's meal plans, if Betsy made her way to the garden to pick the produce. Rising dough for dinner rolls sat on the counter. Miss Woodson recently retired to take a nap for the afternoon so there was time to make the tarts.

She flattened the pastry dough with a rolling pin, cut out small circles with the lip of a glass, and pushed little crusts into a muffin pan. As they baked, she used the double boiler pans to mix the lemons, cornstarch, sugar, and eggs until they were creamy. She blew on the spoon and lifted it to her lips for a taste.

"I smell something delicious." Dale's voice sent a tingle down her spine. She turned without tasting and gazed into his eyes. Her mouth drooled. Whether the salivating came from looking at the man in front of her, or the lemon concoction sliding down her spoon, she wasn't sure. She shoved the spoon into his hand and licked her lemon-coated fingers. They both hummed in satisfaction at the same time.

His gaze turned to her fingers pressed to her lips. She jerked them out of her mouth and stepped away to wash her hands in the sink. When she turned her back to him, she realized the need to take a breath. How embarrassing. He probably put her in the same category as June. She hadn't meant to flirt but hated to admit it felt good. His arm reached around her side, placing the spoon in the sink. She couldn't control the sigh pushing through her chest. She was in trouble if she didn't do something to control her attraction.

She turned and stared at his overalls. The rustic clothing helped remind her of the distance she wanted to maintain. "You're a little early for dinner, country boy. Shouldn't you be at work?"

He stepped back and put a thumb under each side of his shoulder straps. "The plant decided to give everyone an afternoon off each week since production is down. I promised Miss Woodson I'd do some weeding in her garden. Today seemed like the perfect opportunity to complete her wish. I reckon the good Lord has provided some fine produce in your victory garden. Can you point me to the tool shed?"

The slight twang of his voice reminded Betsy of her plans to stay away from all things country. How could she have forgotten his background? She raised her chin and turned toward the oven. "If you follow the path outside the kitchen's back door, it will take you to two sheds. The one on the right has the tools you need." She pulled out the tart shells and reached into a drawer for another spoon. "I have some tarts to make." She started plopping the lemon pudding into the shells. "They need time to cool before the meal."

He laughed as he headed out the door. "Cooling down something tart sounds like a good idea."

A dip coursed through her midsection. Thank the Lord, Dale couldn't see her face. Her parents could always guess her reaction to the world by looking at Betsy's blazing cheeks. She stared out the kitchen window. Seconds later, she saw him striding toward the sheds. He looked comfortable in his casual clothing. For that matter he looked at ease when he wore a dress shirt and tie for his work at the powder plant.

She turned away from the window and finished placing the lemon concoction into the tart crusts. She rinsed her hands and remembered the rest of the things planned for supper. She needed to pick fresh beans and corn. Oh, dear. Another encounter with the country boy would be sure to follow. If only she hadn't promised June the fresh vegetables. The confrontation sure to follow reminded her of the last poem she'd read about Missy and Samuel.

Samuel's Lament/Missy's Rebuttal

Bright tears rained down his stormy face.
"The cities fell, to our disgrace.
We took the homes of war-torn wives,
And burned their towns, or took their lives.

Small children ran and tried to hide.
My conscience died with that day's ride."

I took his hands to offer peace,
He squeezed mine once, then found release.

"I do not want another bride,
Who'd suffer from my cruel side.
I used to care, but now I doubt
I'd show her love, or only shout."

I stood and planted hands on hips.
"I don't believe your angry lips.
Deep down I know your heart still cares,
For those who face our world's despairs."

"But what about the ones I hurt,
Whose only hope lies in the dirt?
I helped to tear their cities down.
Their faces changed from fear to frown."

"Instead of bringing hope to all,
I'm left with memories of their fall.
My missing leg makes me recall,
The painful outcome of the brawl."

"Oh, Samuel, my love, my friend,

This awful war will someday end.
Until that day we must ensure,
Our words of freedom still endure."

"You may have lost a foot to war,
But we can keep an open door.
For those who travel by our way,
And seek a guarded place to stay."

The tears still ran down from his eyes.
"My love for you, I can't disguise,
But will you love me, though I'm lame,
And wounded by this war-filled shame?"

I took his arms and drew him near.
"We all must face our guilt and fear.
For years I treated others wrong
But now God gives my heart a song."

"Reach out and take the Savior's hand,
It's He who helps us understand,
That His forgiveness offers grace,
And sins are gone without a trace."

He took my hands and stood with me.
We faced each other, knee to knee.
Standing on one foot, he stared,
His face had changed, I knew he cared.

He closed his eyes and whispered prayers,
We lifted up our woes and cares.
"Oh, Lord, who guides us through these times,
Forgive our lack of faith, our crimes."

Hope fills my heart for brighter days
I hold him closer as he prays.
Perhaps one day he'll see in me,
A partner who would never flee.

Chapter Thirteen

Dale
1946

Dale shook his head as he fled out the back door. He grew up in a home of mostly men. Ma provided the only feminine influence in their lives. She'd concentrated on teaching her boys morals and manners, but his mother was as hardy as the rest of the family. She had often donned overalls and joined her husband and sons when they farmed the land.

Living in the boarding house with June's flirtations, Margie's dislike, and his confusion about Betsy was new territory. The last few years serving in the military with other men hadn't helped either. He'd avoided the coarse talk in the barracks after having heard things causing his mother's admonitions about morals to beat their way into his conscience. He didn't miss the coarser parts of his years in the service. As he reached the two sheds, he spotted the garden straight ahead. Working the ground again would be a pleasure.

He opened the door to the shed on the right and found several hoes to choose from. One looked freshly sharpened so he grabbed the tool and headed for the vegetable patch. The plot looked well-cared for. As he walked around the edge, he wondered who did most of the work. A few minutes later he located several rows with weeds. He worked quickly and soon had them cleared. The chore brought fond memories of the familiar. Ma and Papa Herbert often sang hymns when they'd all been at home. Without giving his mind a chance to disagree, he began singing "Amazing Grace." He needed some grace for his times of neglecting God during the last few years.

The military had given him a pocket New Testament during his service. There were a few tales about the little book saving someone from a fatal bullet. His faith hadn't been strong enough to believe all the stories were true. He'd stepped back from his once strong belief after news of Joseph's death reached him. There had been no denial of God, only a stepping away.

Dale knew who parted ways. It wasn't the Lord. Sorrow for his brother and survivor's guilt overwhelmed him. Worship became a struggle. He'd avoided it until now. Miss Woodson and his fellow boarders came back from church refreshed each Sunday. The temptation to join them felt as real as the smell of freshly turned soil and the rustle of the corn stalks in the row he had just finished. More than the wind rustled those plants.

Betsy worked on the far side of the corn. He watched as she took her time selecting and pulling ears. The attractive young woman shucked them like a regular farm gal and placed each piece in the pot at her feet. He started whistling an off-tune version of "Beautiful Dreamer" as he approached. There was no need to set her on edge again.

"Hey, Miss Betsy, are we having corn for supper tonight?" He watched her cheeks flame and couldn't stop the grin from forming on his lips.

Her voice was stiff when she answered. Her eyes focused on the task. "Corn will be part of the meal. If you want to make yourself useful, there's another pan for green beans." She pointed to the end of the bean row where a container sat.

He guessed she didn't want his help with the corn. He could take a hint. "I'd be glad to pick the beans. Ma taught me how to get the strings off of them if you want some help once we're done."

Dale glanced her way. He received a nod and a shy smile. Progress. At least she wasn't flirting or hating like the other women boarders. He leaned over and started picking the beans. "So, tell me about your church."

Bean pods pinged off the side of the metal pan. She lifted the full container of corn and moved to the row next to his. Excitement spread across her face. He paused for a moment to admire her looks.

"Our worship services start at eleven. You are welcome to join us. We also have a Sunday school at ten. Most of the boarders go to both."

"I'll have to give it some thought." He would consider going, but he needed to think about his decision.

Her expression grew hopeful. Sweetness washed into his soul. The urge to say yes to her pleading eyes grew.

She must have seen his yearning. Her voice grew in confidence as she revealed more information about the church. "Our minister has been preaching out of the books written by the apostle John. His messages are full of hope. I think you would enjoy them." She paused. Her expression wavered when he didn't respond right away. She bit her lip and moved down the row of beans.

He decided to put her out of her misery. "What time do you leave on Sunday mornings?"

She stopped picking beans and straightened. Her face glowed. "We gather on the porch at Woodson House around nine-thirty and then walk over together. We'd be happy to have you join us."

He hoped he didn't regret his decision. Would making the choice for Betsy's sake be the right reason for going to church or giving God a place in his life?

Scott
Present day

Scott exited the church, surrounded by the other praise band members. He helped out the band every other week these days to spend time with his wife's small church on alternate Sundays. Ginny waited outside the door, chatting with an older actor from her play. Their laughter rang out across the sidewalk, enticing him to hurry to his beautiful wife's side. It took every ounce of strength to keep from blurting out their baby news to his closest friends in the music group. He'd managed to keep his excitement contained when they attended Ginny's home church last Sunday.

During today's worship, Honey, a perceptive grandmother figure to both of them, looked his way with a perplexed expression. She'd raised her eyebrows at him while plucking away on her bass guitar during the praise songs. When she started to say something after church, he'd used the meal with Roy and Mama Jessie as an excuse to leave in a hurry.

Wrapping his arm around his wife, he acknowledged the gentleman with a handshake. "Good to see you, sir. My apologies for interrupting, but Ginny and I promised to be at her mother's home for lunch."

The older man nodded. "You better be on your way then. Keeping the in-laws happy is a smart move, young fellow."

Ginny waved to several of her acquaintances as he pulled her close for their walk to the car.

Scott leaned near her ear. "Are you ready to find out if I have more than one in-law? Maybe your mom and Roy will finally set a wedding date."

She stepped away long enough to grab both his hands. She swept them into a swirling dance and then swayed to a stop. "Whoa. My head's still circling." She let go with one hand and placed the free palm on her forehead.

Fear like a tidal wave slapped at his chest. "Are you okay?" He heard a quiver in his voice.

She looked up, removed her hand from her head, placing it on his arm. "I better stick to slower dancing for the next few months." An almost imperceptible belch made it past her lips. Their eyes met. She shook in laughter as relief slid off his shoulders. He would need a strategy map to follow her changing emotions during her pregnancy. Not that his feelings were any better contained.

The sound of someone else laughing made them both turn.

Honey nudged his hip with the tip of her guitar case. "You two let me know when you're ready to share your news with the rest of us. Until then, mum's or should I say *mom's* the word." She zipped an imaginary zipper across her lips and climbed into her red sports car. "Take care of our Ginny." She gave one final wave and roared out of the parking lot.

"I think we need to talk to her about a new muffler." Scott looked around and was glad no one else overheard their conversation. If he had his way, they'd have shouted the news this morning, but he would respect Ginny's wish to keep things quiet for a while.

"I just hope she will keep her mouth muffled until we are ready to share with everyone."

He hadn't seen a frown on his wife's face in a long time. She would need his reassurance.

"Honey is a wonderful woman who always keeps her promises. You won't need to worry about her. We'll have to make her an honorary great-grandmother when our little one arrives. She's always been a sweetheart to me."

"Yeah, I remember thinking she was your girlfriend at one time." Ginny settled into their car as he held the door open.

Before closing the door, he leaned down to kiss the top of her head. "You are the only girlfriend I wanted. This baby is going to make us one happy family." He closed the door and strutted to the driver's side. He planned to be the proudest papa, if he could make it through the next few hours without spilling their good news.

A short time later, Scott pushed Mama Jessie's doorbell and listened to a chiming song play inside the house. Entering his mother-in-law's abode provided Scott with a new adventure whenever they visited her home.

Jessie Cline was a strong woman. She lived life to the fullest, despite having her first husband desert her and their two children for another woman. Then not long after he left, the man passed away in a tragic automobile accident, leaving them in debt. She had covered her suffering with a positive attitude and hard work. Her enduring spirit provided a loving home for her children.

Mama Jessie answered the door with a smile, wearing a loose multicolored top swinging from side to side when the active woman stopped to wave them in. "Come in, you two, and join the party."

Scott glanced at his wife.

Ginny shrugged. "What kind of celebration are we having today, Mom?"

"Come inside, and you'll find out." The fascinating woman beckoned them in. She'd made a living as a freelance artist while sharing the care of her children with their grandmother. He'd enjoyed hearing Ginny's tales of summers at her Grandma Stuart's home. They both were enjoying the retelling of Great-Grandmother Betsy's life.

"I can hardly wait." Ginny took Scott's arm. They followed her mom down the hallway toward the kitchen. He balanced the tray of lemon tarts in one hand and pulled his wife closer with the other. The hallway wasn't wide. At least it was the excuse he gave himself for wrapping his arm around her trim waist. He tried to control his expression, but knew he beamed with the knowledge her middle might not be so thin in a few months.

"Roy and I have a big surprise for everyone. Your brother is already here, so the whole family will hear our good news at the same time."

"I can hardly wait to find out about the celebration today. Are you ready to share?" Scott hoped it would be the news of the older couple setting a wedding date. He prayed it would be soon and not near the baby's birth.

"Dinner first. I've made all of our favorites, at least the ones I know how to fix." Jessie laughed. Her ability to cook most dishes was limited. "Roy purchased the rest, so everyone should enjoy the meal. Welcome to our feast."

Nathan sat on one side of a table loaded with a smorgasbord of dishes. Ginny and Scott sat facing him, with Jessie sitting at the foot. Roy prayed for the meal from the head seat of the spread. Conversations ranged from mundane to politics, until the time for dessert arrived.

"Thank you for bringing lemon tarts. They will complement the ice cream cake I ordered for our special announcement." Jessie rose and stepped behind Roy's chair. She put her hands on his shoulders. They looked into each other's eyes and then turned to face their audience.

Nathan rubbed his belly. "Let me guess, you're going to write and illustrate a children's cookbook."

Ginny placed a hand on her own stomach and glared at her not-so-humorous brother. "Not funny. Let them make their big announcement."

"We'll be right back with the ice cream cake. The dessert will tell you our news." Jessie and Roy headed for the kitchen. They returned carrying a decorated cake with their names, a wedding cake topper, and the previous Friday's date.

"I think the joke's on us, Sis." Nathan gaped at his mother.

"You eloped?" Ginny's face paled as the older couple grinned and nodded. "You kept your wedding a secret from your children?" She grabbed for Scott's hand. Her palm felt clammy and weak in his grasp. Her head fell forward and she leaned down toward her knees.

"Are you all right, sweetheart?" Scott felt slightly faint as he watched his wife attempt to take deep breaths.

"Just give me a minute." Ginny's voice sounded muffled as she grasped the side of the table and edged her way to a sitting position.

A huff of air pushed its way out of Scott's chest as he wrapped an arm around her shoulders and waited until she raised her head.

"I think they made a good choice to elope, sis. No need to worry about all the expenses of a fancy forty-minute event. You don't have to pass out over their announcement. I've never known you to be a wimp." Nathan stuck a finger into the cake and hummed as he put the treat into his mouth.

"Neither have I." Ginny's mother stepped closer without correcting her son's childlike behavior. She placed a hand on her daughter's forehead. She smiled. Then she sighed. "Maybe you've been keeping a secret of your own."

Ginny laid a hand over her mouth and rushed from the room, leaving Scott to face her family alone. Gagging sounds echoed from the nearby bathroom.

"I uh, we uh... Ginny wanted to wait until she was a little farther along." He swallowed. Did he betray Ginny by speaking up? His mother-in-law's expression faded from a frown to concern. Roy and Nathan looked at each other in confusion.

"Does she have something serious? Should we go to the emergency clinic?" Roy pulled his cell from his pocket.

Scott waved his hand. "There's nothing wrong that a good nine months won't cure."

Recognition spread across the other men's faces. Roy grinned. "I'm going to be a grandpa."

"Guess the birth will make me an uncle. Congrats, Scott. You just took a lot of pressure off me to get married and have a child of my own." Nathan slapped him on the back and handed the cake knife to his new stepfather. "Let's celebrate this wedding and my new nephew or niece."

Jessie frowned at Nathan. "I'm not letting you off the hook, son. Where is the girlfriend you promised to bring today?" Her words implicated her son, but her eyes studied Scott, demanding answers. Ginny had reminded him many times that her mother might not be excited about them having a child so soon after their marriage.

Scott straightened his back and gave her look for look. "We're both excited about our baby. Our plan has always been to have a family as soon as possible."

"Just make sure you take time for each other and any other children who come your way." Jessie's shoulders relaxed when Roy wrapped his arm around her and held their palms around the cake knife.

"I'm pleased to be an official part of this family now, and I'm with Nathan. Let's celebrate our new life together as happily married grandparents of Scott and Ginny's child." Roy nodded toward Scott. A smile covered the older man's face as the newlyweds sliced the cake.

Ginny entered the room, looking pale but beautiful. Her mouth dropped open at Roy's words. Scott shrugged when she looked his way. "Your mother figured out your condition. I admitted the truth. Let's not do anything to mar this wedding celebration."

Chapter Fourteen

Ginny
Present day

After returning home from the day of celebration, Ginny pulled out the poems and sorted through them. She'd seen one about a wedding somewhere in the pack. The fragile papers crackled in her hand, reminding her of the need to buy protective sleeves to preserve the historic documents. She added the purchase to her to-do list for the upcoming week, along with putting the finishing touches on her lessons each night.

Once she found the poetry, she plopped onto the loveseat and raised her feet. "Hey, Scott, I'm reading Missy's poem about her wedding."

"I'll be there in a minute. Your hound just made a mess in the kitchen."

"If I recall, you married me for better or worse. The worse part makes Jezebel your pet, too." Ginny laughed and held the aging document to her nose. She inhaled the aroma of ancient paper with a hint of wood and lavender. While waiting for Scott, she checked her phone for messages. A text from Roy revealed a selfie attachment showing the latest newlyweds standing in front of the courthouse, wearing their Sunday best, and holding a marriage certificate.

Celebrating with Mom and Roy brought back fond memories from her wedding in December. Both marriages and the impending birth of a new family member made the afternoon fly by in a whirl of happiness. They'd called Scott's parents and let them know the good news. They were thrilled about becoming grandparents. Ginny's stomach settled after everyone's happy words of celebration. She'd even recovered enough to enjoy a lemon tart covered in ice cream cake. Having seconds wasn't a problem.

Mom's hesitancy about Ginny having a baby within a year of their marriage faded with Roy's reassurances about loving the whole family. Scott made sure her mom knew he would be an equal partner when it came to parenting. He was busy putting those words into action by taking care of her pet.

Scott came into the room, wiping his hands on a paper towel. After tossing it into a nearby can, he sat next to Ginny. "We need to start putting the chow on a higher shelf. I'm sorry I blamed the mess totally on Jezebel. It seems we've got a couple of scheming pets. They figured out how to open the lower cabinets and have a snack."

"They make quite a team." Her laughter blended with his as the two innocent-looking dogs padded into the room and climbed onto their laps. Ginny held the poem high to protect it from their slobbery kisses.

"So do your mom and new stepdad." Scott twirled a tendril of her hair, sending a shiver down her spine.

"I'm glad they finally married. I wish I could have been there, but I understand they wanted to keep it simple after putting on a big event for us." Ginny fought the urge to pout.

Scott leaned closer. "Let's finish this day of celebrations by reading about Missy and Sam's special day."

Missy 1870

Wedding Day

We had a quiet wedding day.
Our rites were short, without delay.
Sam did not want the gawkers there,
While speaking words that showed his care.

We spoke our vows with few around.
My aunts, the parson, and the sound
Of promises wrapped up with hope,
And prayers to help us both to cope.

With times of woe or loss of wealth,
Through days we'll fill with joy and health,
We spoke our vows with sweet elation,
For our private celebration.

Betsy
1946

After reading about Sam and Missy joining their lives, Betsy flipped to the back of *Lo, Michael*. The final scene in her well-read book described a marriage. In fact, there were two. If her memory served her right, after Michael and Starr's wedding, his friend Sam also married the woman he loved. Sam, in the book, didn't want much. He was glad to have gotten out of the tough neighborhood and found his place on the farm.

Betsy wondered if Missy's Sam struggled to deal with his missing foot or the memories of serving in the war. She'd noticed many returning soldiers from World War II didn't want to talk much about their tours overseas. Dale's scars seemed mostly to come from the loss of his half-brother. His wound might be harder to heal than a physical one since he felt guilty for being the son who lived.

The war affected more than the soldiers. The women at home suffered, too, whether from the change from homemakers to factory workers or in their relationship with a soldier. Ike affected her attitude toward men. She didn't plan on making any quick decisions about love again after his betrayal. Missy and Sam were smart to work through his problems before they entered marriage. Even Sam and Michael, in Hill's novel, survived many tough events before choosing to marry the women they each loved.

Thoughts of Dale filtered into her mind, but she pushed them away. They hadn't known each other long. Besides, she had other plans for her future before tying herself to any man. Pushing his handsome face from her thoughts, she turned her focus to the stack of papers she'd been reading.

She picked up the next poem and noticed a much later date. Missy's marriage to Sam must have taken over her spare time. Unless writings were missing from the large span of time, there was a big gap. The title spoke of graves. The subject sounded ominous. Betsy paused. Then curiosity prodded her to keep reading to discover the story of Miss Woodson's parents, be it good or bad. No life was free from harm. She'd learned the hard way from her former boyfriend, Ike Jones.

Small Graves

Cholera has struck our land.
Took a new child from my hand
Though I'd hoped our Mae would thrive,
Our small child is not alive.

One more Woodson in the ground,
Near her grave is Davy's mound
Heaven bound before he breathed.
Broke our hearts, we sighed and seethed.

Yet we kept our grief inside.
Knew our Father would provide.
Now we work to save our son,
Pray and soothe until we've won.

One day we will all unite,
In a land with heaven's light.
While we have our time on earth,
Maybe we will see new birth.

'Til that time I'll do my best.
Let my Jesus do the rest.
Praise Him for the ones I love.
Look to God, find hope above.

Betsy's heart sank as she read about the deaths of several children. She hoped the couple saved the life of the boy mentioned in the poem. Miss Woodson had mentioned having an older brother, Warren, the father of her niece, Lottie. Missy and Samuel's lives wove a pattern of sadness. Not everyone received a happy life like in June's dreams. It seemed more people faced disappointment. She wiped at the moisture dripping from her nose and hugged her middle as misery swept through her soul.

Ginny
Present day, late March

The cramping started suddenly. Ginny held her belly and fought the pain. The ache of a failed pregnancy passed in a bloody rush to the bathroom. Hope for the future died. Two hours later, she sat in a hospital room, waiting.

Dr. Giles stopped by. He assured them they'd be able to try again, after a quick procedure to make sure her uterus was clean.

His words stabbed at her heart. The sweet baby she longed for no longer existed. Cold streaks of agony chilled her cheeks. Scott sat by her bed holding her hand. She tried to absorb his comfort, but waves of loss overpowered his efforts.

"I'm sorry, sweetheart." He kissed the palm of her hand and held it to his cheek.

Ginny's sobs increased. "Me, too. I wish I knew what I did wrong."

He wrapped his arms around her shaking shoulders. "I don't think you did anything to hurt this baby."

"I'm not sure. Did I do too much lifting when I moved into our house? Was there some flu bug I caught from going to work? Maybe I should have quit work. I've worked so hard to save my job, only to lose our child. I feel so guilty." Tremors shook her body.

Scott's glistening eyes met hers. "There is no need to blame yourself, sweetheart." He bowed his head for a moment before speaking again. "Would you like to see your mother before they sedate you for the procedure?"

Ginny nodded. Scott turned away and went out the door. She shuddered, missing his support. Moments later, her mother stepped near and hugged her close.

"It will be all right, honey. I don't think I ever told you about two miscarriages during my marriage to your father."

"Oh, Mom, how did you ever get over the loss?" Ginny swiped at her eyes and looked at her mother. A shared sympathy rolled through her chest.

"A part of you will always remember, but your marriage is young. You have plenty of time to have other children."

"But this child won't be part of our family." A keening moan rose from Ginny's throat.

"Maybe not in a physical way, but your angel baby will always have a special place in heaven and your heart. Let's have a prayer before the doctor comes." Her mother prayed for Ginny's peace and for the memory of a small soul gathered into the arms of God. Cleansing tears flowed from both women's eyes.

"Thanks, the prayer helped, but I feel so empty on the inside."

"The loss won't go away overnight. Don't be afraid to seek help from others or a counselor. Using my art skills to draw pictures of babies and children brought me some relief. Sadness about my miscarriages led me to using my sweet art babies to reach other hurting hearts. One of the first books I illustrated was for mothers in your situation. I don't know if I ever shared it with you. Maybe I can find a copy." Mom looked out the window. She seemed to be gathering her thoughts. "You might want to journal or write one of your songs."

"I love you, Mom." Ginny took a deep breath. Her heart overflowed with loss, but she cherished how her family surrounded her through the time of mourning.

Mom held her hand and talked about taking Jezebel and Carlos into her home after Scott let her know what happened. Jezebel managed to find an open paint tube and take a bite out of it. "You now have a purple mouthed dog."

Ginny was still half-smiling at her hound's antics when they wheeled her away to the operating room.

Visions of purple pets and children with angel wings danced through her mind as she slowly woke from her drug-induced sleep. "Violet..."

"Did you say something, sweetheart?" Scott's warm breath tickled her ear.

"Violet... If this child lived, I would have called her Violet."

"She would have been a very sweet Violet. What if the baby was a boy?"

"In my mind, she is a sweet baby girl who is now safe in the arms of Jesus."

Scott leaned over and planted a kiss on her forehead. "I love you."

"I love..." Ginny pushed Scott away and heaved into the small bedside container. "Ugh, I don't think being under anesthesia agrees with me. Sorry about my upset stomach."

"I still love you, regardless." Scott wiped some of the explosion from the front of his shirt.

"That's good to know. Uh, you might want to wipe down the right side of your shirt too." Ginny swiped at her mouth with a tissue and then offered the box to her husband. "It looks like we are making a Jezebel-mess of ourselves." They both laughed. "Mom said she got into some purple paint. I guess her doggie antics made me think of the color violet. I'm so sorry…"

Scott hugged her close. "Don't dwell on the 'what ifs.' We have our whole future to fill up with love, laughter, and lots of little ones."

She pushed his soggy shirt-covered chest away. "Maybe we should make use of some of the bibs from the shower last week. Your shirt is getting me all wet." She frowned. "Do we need to return the gifts?"

"I don't think we have to worry about returning anything. We're going to have a child through adoption or through our love. We just have to be patient." He leaned closer with a mischievous grin and blew a raspberry kiss onto her cheek. Stepping away he wiggled his eyebrows, causing her to giggle.

A cheerful voice sounded from the doorway. "I'm glad to see you looking alive and well. The doctor says you're good to go home by this evening. Take it easy for a few days. Then you should be able to resume normal activities by the end of next week." The nurse, who wheeled her away about an hour or so before, now tapped information into her computer on wheels. After checking vital signs, she asked if they needed anything.

"Do you have any ginger ale? My stomach has been a little upset." Ginny fought against another wave of nausea.

"Sure thing, hon. Lots of people have a similar reaction. I'll be right back." The nurse returned moments later with crackers, ice, and a can of the requested soda.

Sipping on the cool drink and eating a few crackers helped settle Ginny's stomach. If only her thoughts were as easy to calm down. She needed to give the loss over to God, but worry threatened to ruin any attempt at peace. Maybe she should take Mom's advice and try to write about the child.

"Did the soda help? Let me know if you need anything else." The nurse eased a warm blanket over Ginny's lap.

"Could I have some paper and something to write with?" Ginny suddenly yearned to put her thoughts into words.

"Let me see what I can find. We're all computerized these days, but I can check at the nurse's station."

Scott cleared his throat. "No problem, I've got a pen and a small pad of paper in my pocket."

The nurse scurried from the room, leaving the couple in privacy.

Ginny picked up the pencil as thoughts swirled in her head. After staring at the paper for a few minutes, she began to pour out her feelings. Scott's hand caressed her back.

Sweet Violet

I loved you, Sweet Violet, dear child of my heart.
I wanted to hold you from your very start,
But now you are held in the hands of our Lord,
And we will not see you until our reward.
I yearn for the days when I'll see your sweet face
And hold your small hand as we sing of God's grace.

The words were few, but a sliver of hope flowed into her spirit as cleansing streams once more coursed from her eyes. "Please heal my hurting, Lord. Take my child to Your heart. I pray someday we can hold another child of our own. It still hurts. I mourn this loss, but I place my trust in You, even if I don't understand."

Scott's arms held her closer as his whispered voice joined her pierced soul in prayer.

~~~~~

Over the next few days, feelings of helplessness began to overwhelm Ginny. She prayed, she wrote, she trusted, and then she doubted. The miscarriage occurred right before spring break. She should be using the time to refresh. Instead, she rode a rollercoaster of emotions as she pulled inwards.

The doorbell rang. Scott's voice echoed down the hall along with older feminine tones. Ginny wanted to curl up under the warm crocheted afghan, hoping to bury her miseries and herself into the cushions of her grandmother's old couch. The approaching footsteps told her trying to hide under her covers would do no good.

Honey's warm voice and the scent of roast beef filtered into the room. Ginny pushed into a sitting position and adjusted the afghan over her pajama-clad body.

"Hi, sweetie, I brought you a beef and noodle casserole." Honey handed the dish to Scott and nestled in next to the younger woman. Her arms wrapped around Ginny's shoulders as they consoled each other. Scott and the dish disappeared from the room as the two mourned Violet's loss.

Once their grief-ridden shoulders stopped shaking, Ginny grabbed the tissue box, and they mopped their faces. "Thank you for coming."
~~~~~

"I love you and Scott. You are my children in spirit."

"You understand what I'm going through, don't you?"

"I do. My husband and I tried for years. After several miscarriages and a cancer threat took away all hope of having a child, we began to seek a different direction. The love we wanted to share with a family turned to caring friendships with older students, and even lonesome college professors, like Scott, who needed the affection their distant parents couldn't provide. The distance came from either physical or psychological reasons. We involved ourselves in the lives of many young folks, who we unofficially adopted into our hearts."

"Did you ever consider adopting?" Ginny's thoughts turned to the papers they needed to complete for the adoption process to start.

Honey's hands fidgeted in her lap as she leaned away. "We gave some thought to adopting, but our professional and private lives became so busy we decided against permanently taking someone into our home. Instead of limiting ourselves to one or two lost souls we opened our home to many."

"Scott and I have our mission to many children through teaching our students. We've known since the beginning of our marriage we also wanted natural and adopted children. Both of us were thrilled to learn of our pregnancy. I feel like a failure. Did my busyness lead to not carrying my baby full-term?"

"I don't..." Honey paused and placed a palm on her forehead. Lowering her hand, she cleared her throat as she wrapped an arm around Ginny. "Only God knows what your future will bring. Why don't we pray right now?"

Ginny nodded and accepted the older woman's comfort. She knew she needed to talk to God, but didn't seem to have the words to say at the moment. Most of Honey's words faded into muffled sounds as Ginny closed her eyes and wept until exhaustion claimed her tired body and soul.

Chapter Fifteen

Dale
1946

Dale closed his eyes as the minister prayed. After deciding to keep his promise to Betsy earlier in the week, he'd joined the boarders on their journey to church earlier in morning. His co-worker, Allen welcomed him into a Sunday school class and now sat on one side of Dale with his family. Betsy sat on the other. The past few days sent shards of worry through his troubled thoughts. Pressure to find his mother's missing treasure and the need to start searching for a new job pestered his mind with concerns for the future.

Working in Miss Woodson's garden and doing yard work wore his body down enough so he could fall into an exhausted sleep each night. Still, the early mornings found his thoughts twisted with worrisome dreams. He silently added a petition for missing answers to the preacher's ongoing prayer. Relief edged into his soul. Taking his cares to the Lord should have been his first step.

The congregation responded with a warm "Amen." Dale opened his eyes to see Betsy pick up a hymnal and offer to share the book. His hand brushed hers when she turned to the announced page number. She looked away, but the pink in her cheeks brightened his day. Moving closer, his voice joined hers as the song of praise soared to heaven. His tenor and her alto harmonized so well, others turned with nods and smiles.

He tried to focus on the words but couldn't resist a quick look at his singing partner. Her eyes drifted closed as she sang the well-known words. She looked angelic. Her voice flowed with words about the church's one foundation being Jesus. A yearning to draw closer to the young woman opened a closed door in his heart. After the song ended, they sat to listen to the message for the day.

"Cast all your cares and fears on the Lord. The Bible states clearly the need to take the things weighing us down to God. He is our true Father and cares for us like we are His sons and daughters." The minister's words settled into Dale's mind, reinforcing the need to give his plans to the Holy One. He bowed his head and thanked his Heavenly Father for the words he heard and the worship service lifting his spirit. He should have come sooner, but God's timing was perfect. More words followed about not being afraid to ask God for help and being open to His leading.

When the final song ended, he turned to Betsy, ready to ask a few questions without fear. "Would you walk back to the boarding house with me?"

She shrugged, but fell in beside him after they exited the church. "I'm glad you came to church with the rest of us today."

"I am too. I'm sorry I waited so long to get back where I belong. The war distracted me from doing the right things. From now on, I'll be here every Sunday, at least until the powder plant closes down."

"Do you know what will happen then?" The yearning in her voice gave him courage to share his thoughts.

"I've been worried, but after today's sermon, I feel inspired to trust in God's timing. I've sent out a few letters of interest for other jobs in several cities, but no one has answered. I reckon I can always go back and work the farm with Papa Herbert."

Betsy's expression showed interest in his plans until he mentioned the farm. Since he was feeling inclined to find answers, he decided to ask about her frown. "Do you have a problem with me going back to help at the farm?"

She crossed her arms and stepped back. "You can do whatever you want with your life. Your plans are not my concern."

"But you started frowning when I mentioned going there. Do you want me to stay here with you, or do you just hate farming?" Hope rose in his heart.

She relaxed her arms and clasped her hands as she looked away. "I lived on a farm most of my life. After working for Miss Woodson as her secretary, I have dreams of a career in a city and never having to get my hands dirty again."

"So, you didn't answer the part of the question about me leaving." Dale couldn't resist winking at the cute woman.

"You can wipe the smile off your face, Mister. If you are looking for someone to date, you better start paying attention to June. She is more than interested. I opened my heart once and got burned." She hurried down the walkway.

Dale hustled to keep up with her. "I'm sorry about your bad experience. Do you want to talk about the guy?"

"His name was Ike Jones. I thought he loved me. We got engaged right before he shipped off for overseas duty."

"Did he get killed?" His question halted her steps.

"Death would have been too good for him. I became so enamored by his attention, I failed to see he dated more than one girl while he was here."

"I'm sorry you were hurt. At least you didn't marry him and find out about his unfaithfulness when it was too late."

"I am glad we didn't marry, but my trust in men was damaged. Our relationship ended with a letter. His final message broke my heart. I don't know if I'll ever be ready to date anyone again. I've got bigger plans in the city."

Disappointment rolled through Dale's mind. His brother had often acted like Ike and left a trail of broken hearts behind. She was right. They didn't need to complicate the friendship they'd established during his hunt for treasure. "Thank you for being willing to share. I won't bring up Ike or his letter again. I'm going to go exploring in the basement once we get to Woodson House. Are you up for some treasure hunting?"

Scott
Present day

Scott stared at the latest email. In all the excitement and disappointment, he'd forgotten to set up an observation required by the school. He was a week late. If the evaluation didn't occur immediately, his hunt for the treasured tenure track position would be impossible. His supervisor's message suggested the observation take place tomorrow afternoon. The requisite paperwork was due before then. No excuses. He taught a full load of classes in the morning. It looked like he'd pull an all-nighter and then need an optimal performance teaching his afternoon class in front of the department chair. With no other choice, he sent a response to his superior, Amber Whitney, and started on the required forms and detailed lesson outline.

"Are you coming to bed soon?" Ginny leaned against the doorframe with a wistful look on her face.

"I wish I could. Professor Whitney just sent a reminder about missing a deadline needed for staying on track for tenure. I'd rather be with you, but I've got a bunch of paperwork and lesson plans to type before morning. Fortunately, the good professor was willing to extend the due date by a few more hours. My mind has been focused on other things lately."

Scott turned back to the computer. The sound of a sigh came from Ginny as she padded down the hallway, sending a cloak of guilt to his shoulders. His sweet wife needed him. She'd been through so much, but he needed to succeed in his job to help provide for their future. He ran a hand across his bristly chin and focused on getting his tenure.

Around one in the morning, Scott hit the send button. He flopped back in his chair, hoping he hadn't missed anything. He made his way to their bedroom. After donning some plaid pajama pants, he slid into bed next to his wife. Ginny snuggled closer. He wrapped his arm around her and fell into a sleep tangled with dreams of doubt and dread.

The alarm sounded all too early. After he fumbled to turn off the blaring noise, the scent of Ginny's cinnamon-flavored French toast forced him to open his eyes. He pushed out of bed, heading for the warm meal. A full breakfast would provide extra strength for the challenging day ahead.

"Good morning, sunshine. Thanks for making breakfast." He kissed her cheek before settling into a chair.

"I figured we both could use a hearty breakfast today." She pulled a warm platter loaded with sausage and French toast from the oven. His plate sat next to a pitcher of heated syrup.

"Thanks, sweetheart, I appreciate having a warm meal to keep me going. I stayed up until early this morning." After saying grace, he paused. "Is something going on with you today?"

"Yeah, most of the teachers and other levy supporters are planning to meet tonight. We need to go over how well the campaigns are going and see if we have any other ideas to help gain the vote."

"Are you sure you feel up to going to a stressful gathering?"

"I went back to teaching last Monday. I've dealt with school stress just fine." She laid her palms flat on the table.

"And then you come home ready for bed every afternoon." He reached out with a hand to cover one of hers.

"Today, I felt well enough to fix your breakfast." Her light-hearted grumble spoke heavily of the truth associated with physical loss and heartache.

Scott wrapped an arm around her and stole a kiss. He heard her tummy rumble as she relaxed against him. "Then we better get busy and eat our meal before it gets cold."

The food was delicious. After a cup of coffee, Scott was ready to face his day. "If all goes well during the follow-up review, I should be home in time to eat supper with you. How about we grab some fast food? Then I'll drive you to your meeting."

The smile he received made his day. If he could make it through the next sixteen hours, he'd be dancing around in circles or falling over in a stupor.

His morning classes passed in a whirlwind. When he sat down to open his lunch, a note from Ginny slid out.

Dear Scott,

You are an amazing man. I'm sure you will make your lesson presentation one of the best your supervisor has ever seen. Break a leg on your classroom stage, and don't let the drama of worry bring you low.

Hugs and kisses,

Ginny

Peace soothed Scott's soul as he gained strength from her praise and from the cold chicken sandwich, apple, and chips she'd fixed for him. He'd forgotten about usually packing their lunches together, due to staying up late. He had figured his lunch would be the emergency peanut butter crackers in his desk. His meals as a single man often consisted of snack food. Being married sure provided plenty of advantages. Supporting her tonight at the meeting was the right thing to do. His sweet wife would not need to face the meeting without him. Brushing off a few crumbs, he reviewed his outline one last time and headed for the observation, hoping he didn't cry after the event.

Ginny
Present day, April

A few weeks later, Ginny didn't know whether to cry or lash out at someone. Hitting her head against the wall might be an option, if her head wasn't pounding already. After spending most of the day in a classroom full of anxious students reacting to a real fire drill, due to a small kitchen fire, she'd stayed on her feet all evening. Knocking on doors and talking to resistant people about the levy did not fit anything near what she'd dreamed of when she'd chosen to be a teacher.

Debris littered her home. She'd forgotten to feed Jezebel and Carlos. Scott now spent every Monday and Tuesday evening with the new committee his supervisor required for any hope of tenure. He didn't bother to come home today and care for the dogs or let them out, either. She'd seen more of their pets than her husband in the last few weeks. In addition to the beasts howling and yapping for food, a big puddle oozed across the floor near the back door. Paw prints from the wet spot spread the mess around the kitchen. The scent of urine enveloped the room.

"Stop it." Ginny glared at the animals as they circled her.

She pushed the dogs away with her foot. Jezebel whimpered. Carlos growled. Ginny sank into a kitchen chair and sobbed. Her shoulders heaved as she leaned over the table. Uncontrollable tears rolled from her eyes and soaked her sleeve as she rested her head on her arms.

Moments later, a heavy wet hound muzzle plopped down on her foot. Carlos tapped at her knee with his tiny paws. She picked him up and held him close as she rubbed the top of Jezebel's head. Her chest convulsed as she tried to take a deep breath.

"Please, Lord. I need Your help. I don't even know what to ask of You. I'm so lost and confused." Her voice echoed in the empty room. Doubts about her prayers going beyond the ceiling threatened to overwhelm her heart. The tears started again. She forced herself to feed the dogs. After letting them out for a quick outside run, she threw a towel over their accident. Once they were back inside, she headed for bed without cleaning up the mess or changing. All she wanted to do was curl up and have another cry.

After an undetermined length of time, she heard Scott enter the room. A sob escaped. Tears poured out again despite her effort to control them.

"What's the matter?" Scott's hand rubbed a slow circle on her back. A fountain of loss exploded into her pillow.

Ginny gulped air. Her words tore from her throat in bursts of agony. "I don't know what to do."

Her fist gripped the pillow. "I'm a failure at campaigning. I can barely control my students."

She sobbed harder when Scott pulled her close to his chest. "I couldn't even carry our child full-term."

Moisture from his tears dripped into her hair. "It wasn't your fault, Ginny. I should have been more helpful or insisted you take it easy."

Her need to comfort him overcame the urge to curl into a ball.

"Oh, Scott, it wasn't your fault either. I know our daughter is in God's hands. I'm just feeling so overwhelmed right now. I feel like we never really got to mourn our sweet Violet because of all the school politics."

"I think we need a break from those politics." Scott rested his forehead on hers. He closed his eyes and brushed his lips across her cheek. They both heaved a deep breath and shed a few more tears for their loss. "Thank You, Lord, for the hope our Violet brought us. Help us to remember and look to the future."

Scott's short prayer broke through Ginny's scattered thoughts.

She pushed up into a sitting position. "I think I'd like to start a memorial. Maybe something to bring peace to parents who have suffered a loss like ours?"

"Isn't there a houseplant called violet? Maybe we could send violets, or a craft featuring pictures of the flower so they can remember their little flowers, never growing to full term." He kissed her hand. "I'll bring you one of those plants tomorrow, if I can find any at the florist."

A spark of hope fluttered in her heart, along with a touching memory. "The idea sounds sweet. I remember my grandmother had a shelf spanning two windows. She covered the board with violets. When she wanted a new one, she would take a leaf, place it in moist soil and a new plant would grow from roots the leaf created. I helped her keep them watered when I stayed with her in the summer." Fresh tears threatened Ginny's eyes. "I miss Grandmother Stuart, too."

"I feel like we've been so busy there hasn't been much time to just think and process all the events happening in the last year or so. We put on a massive musical. Our courtship and romance went by in a flash. On top of everything, we were both teaching full-time. Now your job security is on the line. I've been so busy trying to win tenure I've neglected to pay much attention to what you've been going through."

"Don't forget about our plans to adopt and... And our precious lost child, Violet, our desire to give violets..." Ginny choked back a fresh round of weeping. "Why haven't we been able to conceive again? Is there something wrong with me?"

"Maybe it's the stress of everything we're trying to do. Perhaps it's time to step back from something."

"But what? Everything seems to need our attention right now."

"We do have someone who can help."

"I've got Mom and Roy calling people about the school situation. Your parents are mailing postcards to voters. My two best friends are out knocking on doors every day after school."

"What about God?"

"I've tried praying. I tend to fall asleep and not finish my prayers. I'm just so worn out."

"I know what you mean. It seems like I haven't finished a prayer in a long time. Let's pray now."

He wrapped his arms around Ginny. His warmth flowed into her heart. She leaned against his chest. The rumble of his voice made her yearn for the peace Scott prayed for. She added a silent plea of her own as the conviction to take a step back from everything overwhelmed her thoughts.

"Thank you, Scott. I think I need to take a day off tomorrow. I laid everything out at school for tomorrow's classes before I left work today." Saying her plans out loud eased a weight from her shoulders. "It is a Friday, so I can take a long weekend to just mourn and maybe sort priorities." She grabbed a tissue and wiped her eyes before blowing her nose. "Sometimes a teacher needs a mental health day. Maybe after some time off, I will know what I should do."

Scott cleared her damp tissues, placing them in a nearby trash can. He sat next to her and brushed his hands over her hair. "I'm done by mid-morning. I can come home early and try to help you around the house. I'll tell my supervisor we've done enough committee planning for this week."

"It would be nice to have someone to talk to while we sort through things. I'm still unpacking boxes from the move. I haven't touched my grandmother's manuscript or the poems in weeks."

"Then we'll have to take some time out to chill on the couch and read. Why don't we get her manuscript now?" He offered his open arms. As his fingers laced with hers, a flood of calmness rushed over her. She leaned against him, welcoming his kiss.

After a sweet break, they sat in the study, peering over her

grandmother's manuscript.

Chapter Sixteen

Betsy
1946

Betsy peered over Dale's shoulder as he carefully sanded the mortar around another brick. "Do you see any evidence of the hidden room?"

"No. I'm beginning to think the construction crew eliminated the dragon's den when they rearranged the basement." He stepped back and stared at the wall.

She edged past him to sweep the dust from the floor. "At least this basement is cleaner than I've ever seen it before. I think we've poked and prodded every brick and every corner. There doesn't seem to be anywhere else to explore."

"Maybe we're missing some clue. Do you think Miss Woodson's mother might have left a hint in the dragon den upstairs? Have you ever searched through everything in the pantry?"

"Since the other women started helping with the meals, I haven't been in there for a while. I never looked for information about a hidden den when I used the room every day." Betsy scooped the dust into a pan and dumped it in a trash container near the wringer-washer. "Maybe we should check it out today."

He waved toward the stairway. "Lead the way. Let's go face the beast."

Betsy laughed and headed up the steps, pointing the broom like a dragon-slaying lance. Dale's presence behind her bolstered her excitement over what would be a mundane chore of sorting through cabinets. They wandered through the living and dining rooms and then pushed on the door to the slim room off the kitchen. Metal clanged as they struggled to access the room. Betsy no longer laughed. What had happened to the usually organized space?

"I think the dragon is trying to keep us out of his den." Dale's attempt at a joke thudded on the frustration building in Betsy's brain.

"More like a princess named June who doesn't like to clean up after herself." Betsy recalled Margie complaining several times about the woman's clutter after the two women moved into the same room.

Dale tugged gently on Betsy's elbow, sending shivers of delight down her spine. "Let me see if I can reach around the door and move the blockage out of the way."

She hugged her arms around her middle as emotions warred

between frustration over the hidden mess and the pleasure she experienced from his touch. The desire to deny any reaction to the country boy soldier turned scientist added to her confusion. Watching his broad shoulders stretch around the half-open door did not help keep her mind focused on ignoring his good qualities, physical or otherwise. When the door opened, a flood of air released from her chest in a loud gust. She hadn't realized she'd stopped breathing until it rushed out.

"Your castle awaits, my lady." He beckoned her into the room with a quick bow.

She didn't want to think about the color of her face as she scurried into the galley-sized room. Instead, she turned to sort scattered pans back into their rightful places.

"Do you have any idea about where we should search for clues?" Dale looked out of place in the room packed with pots, pans, dishes, and knick-knacks.

"I'm not going to be able to think of anything until I get this stack of pans put away. June needs a quick lesson in housekeeping before she finds someone to marry." Betsy wanted to raise her hands in disgust. Instead, she continued arranging the misplaced cookware. She grabbed a pot and attempted to place it high on a shelf in the built-in cabinet.

Dale took the saucepan from her hands and lifted it over her head onto the shelf. She stepped away, fighting the warmth flowing through her body. He put his hands in his pockets. Coins jingled as he glanced around the room. Then his gaze connected with hers, reawakening the unwanted attraction.

"If there is a clue, my guess would be we should look through the stacks of dishes or bowls that haven't been used in a long time. Ma always has some things hidden away in an old cookie jar. Maybe Missy or Miss Woodson forgot about where the treasure was left."

Betsy nodded and attempted to focus on their goal. "Forgetting sounds like a reasonable excuse. Most of the daily use items are near the door where we came in. I suppose we should start looking for clues over by the window." As she studied the sun-covered shelves at the far end of the pantry, her eyes fell on the neglected row of houseplants. Miss Woodson would be saddened if her African violet collection didn't survive the lack of water. "You can get started looking for treasure. I need to get the watering can and give these plants a drink."

Ginny
Present day

"I really like the idea of giving African violets to those who have gone through a miscarriage. I wish we had time to get the movement started."

Ginny raised her hands in a helpless gesture as she paced their study.

"We can't do everything by ourselves." Scott stopped her pacing and gripped her hands.

"You're right. I want to do something, but I feel so vulnerable, overwhelmed, and maybe ashamed." Ginny released one of his hands to swipe a tissue across her cheeks.

"Those closest to us know what happened. They love us. There is no shame in something we don't have control over." He pulled her closer and wrapped his arms around her.

"But where do we go from here? I would feel bad asking for help." Warmth from his chest covered her worries with comfort.

"Why don't you start with Honey? There's a reason she took me in as a so-called grandson. She freely admits trying to have children but never having a successful pregnancy. Perhaps you two have more in common than you think."

Help was there for the asking. All she needed to do was accept it. Honey mentioned her own loss when she brought over a casserole. Doing things alone came easier than accepting assistance for Ginny. She'd been a loner since her father left the family. Life started to change once she married, and even before, especially during the production of the musical. She often endured a strained relationship with God because she wanted to be in charge.

"You're right. I can't do this alone." A river of relief flowed through Ginny. Admitting she needed help seemed to open the floodgates to possibilities. "I wonder if Annabelle would be interested in doing a podcast about the Violet Project." She sank down onto the worn love seat.

Scott picked up Ginny's phone from the old wooden desk and placed the device on her palm. "You'll never know unless you ask."

~~~~~

"Welcome to Annabelle's Answers. For our discussion today, we are tackling miscarriages, a tough subject many women have endured since the beginning of time. I am your host, Annabelle, and my special guest is Ginny Hallmark. You might remember her from an interview earlier this year when we spoke about the ongoing school campaign. Today she is here about her recent experience with a miscarriage. I offer my sympathies over your loss, sweet lady."

Ginny swallowed her fear and managed to croak out a reply. "Thank you, Annabelle. This has been a rough spring for our family. We yearn for the day when we will have a full-term pregnancy, but right now, we want to help others who have also endured a miscarriage."

Annabelle nodded and smiled her reassurance. "I, too, experienced this in my own life when I was of childbearing age. In fact, I looked up some statistics and over twenty percent of pregnancies end in a
~~~~~

miscarriage during the first trimester. Some studies even went as high as forty percent. So you are not alone in your experience. I'm sure there are many in this listening audience who can attest to this tragedy."

Ginny's voice grew stronger as she continued the conversation. "I want young families to know they aren't alone. When we experienced our miscarriage, we suffered sadness over our lost child, Violet. Since then, we've discovered family and friends who also knew this loss, some more than once."

Annabelle leaned closer to the microphone. "I understand. Many years have passed since our miscarriage. There are days I still wonder about the child who might have been part of our lives. For those who are hurting, don't be afraid to seek someone to help you through the dark times. There are counselors and ministers who would be glad to hear your sorrows. On a happier note, I hear Ginny has chosen to use the African violet flower as part of her outreach to other hurting families."

"Yes, we have chosen the plant partially because it bears our child's name, but also because of how you propagate the violet. They grow by tearing a stem from the mother plant. There are still days where I feel like a part of me was ripped away, but now I can remember my sweet Violet in a different way."

"Can you explain this a little further?" Annabelle's encouragement gave Ginny the strength to continue.

"Yes. To grow another violet, one simply needs to plant the broken leaf and stem in rich soil. Soon the hope of a new plant is born. This is why we have chosen to use the violet as our symbol. We plan to use the plant in our outreach to other mothers and fathers who have experienced a miscarriage. We pray the gift of the flower will bring them comfort as they mourn the child torn from their lives and give them hope for the future. Our desire is someday their hearts may grow to welcome another child through birth, adoption, or just loving the other children around them."

"Thank you for sharing about this project. Do you have a plan for growing and distributing your plants, Ginny?"

"We are going to need everyone's help. We hope volunteers will grow and distribute violets. Friends of those suffering from the aftereffects of a miscarriage can contact us or take the initiative to find or purchase a violet on their own to share a little hope. Doctors cannot share sensitive information about patients with the public. We can't do this on our own. No one could. We just want to get the idea started and help a few along the way. Simply give an African violet or another flower to show you care, so those who've gone through a miscarriage won't feel alone."

"So you aren't planning on starting a business or non-profit to support this concept?"

"I'd like to think of it more as a national or worldwide movement to bring hope to those in mourning, though I am starting a row of new violet plants." Ginny knew the audience couldn't see her, but a heavy weight fell from her shoulders, giving her peace.

"Our thoughts and prayers go out to Ginny and all of you who lost a child this way. We hope our listeners will share a violet with a suffering soul. Who knows, maybe this idea will be a viral hit on social media and set a trend for giving to others. Have a wonderful day, and thank you for listening to Annabelle's Answers Podcast."

~~~~~

"I listened to your podcast with Annabelle the other day." Honey's bass guitar case bumped against Ginny's side as they exited church the following Sunday. "I think you have a great idea. I started spreading the news about it on my social media pages and in our Sunny Seniors Online Group. I got some great responses. There were many likes and forwards of my post."

"Thanks, Honey. I appreciate you sending out the message." The older woman's ability to use modern technology amazed Ginny.

"It was my pleasure. In fact, I started a few new violet plants the other day." Honey popped the trunk of her red mustang and set her instrument case carefully into the open space.

"I didn't realize you grew violets."

Was there anything the woman couldn't do?

"I've got more than one type. My departed husband gave me pink, purple, and variegated ones during our life together." She pressed her hand to her heart and paused before continuing. "You may not have seen the plants because they grow best in my bedroom window."

"That explains why I missed them. Is there a special reason they grow better in your bedroom?" Ginny watched the woman's animated face.

"The window in the room faces mainly north, and they seem to like the angle of the sun."

Both women leaned against the sports car and faced the sun together. The days were getting brighter as the season edged toward spring. The warmth soaked into Ginny's skin as she formed the courage to speak with Honey. Scott had stayed in the building for a church committee meeting. Now was the time to open up to the older woman.

"I never did thank you properly for bringing over food for us after our hospital visit. You did so much for me by letting me mourn with you. I was upset with God, and to be honest I'm not really sure what you said in your prayer for me then. My apologies to both you and my Savior because of what I was going through."

"You have nothing to worry about, sweetie. I think you handled your loss better than I did when my miscarriages happened. My husband and I both railed against God and His wisdom when we realized there was no
~~~~~

hope of a baby in our lives."

"But you survived to touch many lives, including my own. I am thankful for your overcoming faith and willingness to share your love. I want you to know your example helped me reconnect with the Lord."

Betsy
1946

A bell sounded from Miss Woodson's room. The woman normally didn't need to see her companion this time in the afternoon. It was a good thing she and Dale finished their search of the pantry cupboard last weekend. Ancient dishes all sparkled from a thorough dusting, but they found no clues. The only treasure from the venture was a growing friendship with the kind man. Dale seemed to touch her heartstrings any time he came near. Too bad his future didn't seem secure. Besides, she wanted more out of life than being a housewife, especially if the future involved anything other than living in a city.

Betsy stretched. She'd finished up all of Miss Woodson's correspondence earlier in the day. She'd done some dusting in the main gathering spaces and checked on the roast the other gals left in the oven to cook slowly. The aroma of seared beef, carrots, and potatoes scented the house. Her tummy gurgled in anticipation of the evening meal as she put her dust rag into a laundry basket and made her way through the house to see what her employer wanted.

"Did you need me to type another letter?" Betsy set the laundry basket near the door and drew closer to her employer.

"No, I have a surprise for you, my dear." Miss Woodson grinned from ear to ear as she rose from her chair and headed into the closet at the back of her small bathroom.

Betsy followed her until she reached the bathroom door and stopped when the older woman stepped behind the curtain leading to the inner storage room. *Crash.* "Are you all right?"

"I'm fine, honey, just looking for a little adventure."

"In your bathroom closet? Finding an escapade in this cramped space would be surprising for sure." Betsy leaned into the tiny quarters and gently led the woman out of the small space.

Miss Woodson swiveled around at the bathroom door and dusted imaginary particles from her arms. "No, sweet pea, I need my suitcase. You and I are going on a trip."

"Me? Going on a trip? What are you thinking? Someone will need to stay and take care of Woodson House and the boarders." Betsy positioned herself between her employer and the closet.

"Don't worry about this house. June and Margie will be able to manage fine without our interference. They've been doing a fair job keeping up with the kitchen. They should be able to handle the laundry as well as anyone else. Dale and Paul are here to fix the house if anything goes awry."

A twinge of curiosity entered Betsy's chest. She stepped into the storage area and began looking in earnest for the suitcase hidden deep in the closet. By the time she removed several boxes from the space, her desire to join Miss Woodson had grown. She set a box on the toilet and turned with a smile on her face. "Okay, you have my interest. Where are we going?"

"We're going to the biggest city I know about. You need to find out if a metropolis is where you really want to live the rest of your life. My grand-nephew and his wife have invited us to come and visit them in New York City." The older woman leaned against the bathroom doorframe, opposite the closet, a grin on her face.

Suspicion made Betsy place her fisted hands on her hips. "They suddenly decided to have us come?" Something wasn't adding up in her mind.

"Well, Lottie's son seemed glad to have us for a week, after I suggested it might be a good idea." A smirk spread further across her face as she admired her fingernails. "You'll like Woody and Maxine."

"Maybe you should go on your own. I don't want to impose on their family." The whole situation reeked of a masterminded plot to push Betsy into Dale's farm-loving arms and away from her city dreams.

"Nonsense, their daughters are off to college. They have plenty of room in their apartment." She waved her arms and pointed beyond Betsy. "Ah-ha, I see the bags, but they're on the bottom of a stack. Pull them out, one for you and one for me."

Betsy rearranged the closet items and placed the requested suitcases on the floor of Miss Woodson's room. In spite of her protests, a bubble of excitement coursed through her. New York was the largest metropolitan area she knew of, and now they were going to see it in person. She opened one of the cases and laid it on her employer's bed. "How many outfits should we pack?"

"I suppose a week's worth should work. We can do laundry if needed. Put in some everyday dresses and a few nicer ones for church or dining out."

Betsy hated the idea of costing her employer any extra expenditure. "Dining out will be expensive, Miss Woodson. I don't want you to use up all your money on fancy food."

"Who said I'd be using up my money? If you want to live in the city, you will need to budget accordingly. I'll give you your regular salary for the week, but you might want to bring along some of your savings for eating out or purchasing some store-made dresses."

The thought of using her savings nagged at Betsy's dreams of living in the city. Surely she could budget well enough to live on the salary. "I'll be frugal, Miss Woodson. My salary should cover everything I need." She'd offer to cook some of their meals at the nephew's home if money got too tight. She had no immediate need for new clothing.

"We'll be near the best stores, my dear. You might need to consider updating your wardrobe. I'm sure all the city girls are wearing ready-made clothing these days. We might even find some nice hose, since the war is over."

Betsy felt heat rise to her cheeks at the mention of the leg coverings. Unlike the other girls, she'd opted for simple cotton anklet socks for her feet throughout the years of Depression and war. June went so far as to paint a seam on her legs to make it look like she wore a pair of hose, but not Betsy. "I don't think I need any new outfits right now. I made several dresses during the past year."

"If you have your mind set on city life, you will need to dress accordingly." Miss Woodson pulled a stack of undergarments from her dresser and plopped them into her suitcase. She pointed to the other piece of luggage. "Now take your bag and get packed. We are leaving early tomorrow morning."

"I hope I don't regret this," Betsy muttered and headed up the stairs to her little room. As she folded clothes into the bag, thoughts crossed her mind about possibly purchasing a dress or two. Though she prided herself in being a good seamstress, it might be nice to have something a little fancier if she went for a city job interview in the future. Reaching deep into the back of her closet, she pulled out a well-hidden box containing her meager savings. She removed some of the money and placed it in her purse.

Excitement warred with her worries. She was going to New York City, the setting of the book, *Lo, Michael*. She placed her packed suitcase and handbag near her door and picked up the novel. Would Miss Woodson's nephew live in a mansion like the townhouse where Michael's benefactor lived? If so, would there be maids who would be more her equal than the family they'd be visiting? A shiver shook her as thoughts about the ghetto where the hero of the book worked and lived wormed their way into her soul. Novels were overdramatic. Surely the city wasn't too bad. She picked up another poem to keep her thoughts off the upcoming city visit.

Chapter Seventeen

Ginny
Present day

Ginny surveyed her classroom with a critical eye. The space looked really bad. She'd neglected it over the last month or so. Hopefully, her students hadn't suffered from a lack of attention.

Today would be a good day for a spring cleaning, starting with the pile on her desk. Worksheets older than a week went into the recycle bin. The ones from last week deserved a cursory look, but a quick check would be good enough. She knew her student's abilities and what their needs were. Those papers quickly followed the others into the waste heap.

It was time for a fresh start. She pulled down decorations from a bulletin board and replaced the faded background paper with a sunny yellow. As students entered the classroom, rather than passing out more copied activities, she asked them to clean out their desks. The trash can soon overflowed with everything from old snack wrappers to broken pencils. After the students completed the cleaning chore, she instructed them to start a list of words about new beginnings.

Ginny also offered her students the option of choosing words associated with springtime. She decided they'd use those words as a springboard for a poem or collage later in the day. Noise from the students almost covered the final arrival bell, but Ginny noticed the clock at the right moment. She rang her classroom chimes, and the noise settled long enough for her to take attendance. Most of the students had already moved their magnetic name tags to indicate their choice for lunch, so Ginny tapped those numbers into the computer for the kitchen crew. She added her name to the list for a teacher's meal. She'd not bothered to fix lunches for the day, and neither had Scott. They both needed a break. Today, her students deserved a little time off too.

Then it hit her like an armload of textbooks on an open-toed sandal. Melissa didn't answer during roll call. She hoped nothing bad happened at the child's foster home. Usually, Melissa showed up first thing in the morning, wanting to get a hug from her teacher. A twinge of guilt crossed Ginny's mind as she hit *save* on the computer's attendance app. Two months ago, the girl's absence would have been the first thing she noticed. Her priorities had gotten all out of whack. She'd give Melissa's foster parents a call at lunch break to make sure all was fine.

She strolled around the room and noted most children had full pages of ideas. Some words were doodled in balloon letters, while others were barely legible. Maybe it would be good to take those future poems into a lesson on handwriting or choosing a creative font on the computer. She'd give them their choice, after the handwriting lesson. A couple of the students had issues with fine motor control, so allowing them the technology choice would provide for individualization of the final project.

The morning flew by in a flurry of fun. Before creating their written assignment, the class walked around the playground's perimeter and noted the early signs of spring. They shared rough drafts with one another and made improvements. Ginny opened up cabinet doors and pulled out the materials needed for collages. She also found a few watercolor sets and white paper for the children to choose from. Some used their own colored pencils and markers. By the end of the morning, the yellow bulletin board overflowed with students' poems, paragraphs, creative collages, paintings, and drawings.

Each child shared their written words orally and described the meaning behind their artwork. Ginny's heart filled with pride from their accomplishments. She let them know her thoughts. Their beaming faces lifted her soul like a soaring bird. The elation lasted until she dropped them in the cafeteria and headed back to make her call to the home of Melissa's foster parents. She dialed the well-known number and waited for someone to answer.

"Russell home, how may I help you?" The woman's voice sounded strained.

"This is Ginny Cline-Hallmark from school. I'm checking in to see if all is well with Melissa, and if I can do anything to help."

A shaky sob sounded over the line. "Hey, Ginny, I've been expecting your call. We've all experienced a rough time the last twenty-four hours. I'm afraid there's been a couple of disturbing things that have come up. My husband's job is moving out of state. Our new location will change our standing in the foster system here."

Ginny's hand went to her cheek. What would happen to Melissa? She refocused on the phone call.

"And, Melissa's mother has asked for another chance at custody. Unfortunately, both conversations were overheard last night by our girl. No one got much sleep. She is understandably upset, so I decided to keep her home from school for the day."

The floor seemed to drop out from under Ginny's feet. She pulled the nearest student chair closer to the phone and plopped into it. Her fingers twisted the cord on the classroom landline. "I'm so sorry to hear about both troubles. I guess I should reword my comment. You two are going to be missed." She paused before going on. "Has Melissa's mother shown any improvement?"

"Some steps forward, but not enough in my opinion. The last supervised visit ended in coarse words. How about you? Did you ever decide to complete the foster care or adoption papers?" Chelsea Russell's voice grew quieter.

Ginny paused. A wave of pressure threatened to put her in the place she'd been a few days before resolving to be at peace. "We've almost gotten the adoption papers ready. We're hoping for a child like Melissa, but know it is a long shot. Our life has also been a little turbulent lately."

"Maybe you should fill out the foster care application too. I have a feeling Melissa might need you in about a month. We only have four weeks before we leave the area. All the other foster families in this area have a full load. She'd have to be moved from everything familiar, unless someone steps up to help."

Ginny swallowed as she stared at the new bulletin board. Did she dare start something new? "I'll have to talk to Scott before we make any decision. I can only promise to discuss the situation with him at this point."

"I wouldn't have expected any other answer. Now, Ginny, I mean, Mrs. Hallmark, can you tell me what Melissa needs to do in order to catch up with the class after missing today?"

"It's all about a new start."

Betsy
1946

The ground vibrated as Betsy waited next to Miss Woodson at the depot. The engine pulling a line of passenger cars puffed out black coal-scented steam clouds and slowed with a loud hiss. The blast of a horn echoed across the platform and bounced back from the side of the wooden framed building where they'd purchased tickets. A breeze from the slowing train ruffled her skirts as Miss Woodson wrapped her fingers around Betsy's elbow.

The old woman's hand tightened into a firm squeeze. "Are you ready for a new start, Betsy?"

She nodded as Miss Woodson continued chatting. "I'm excited to be traveling again. Back in the teens, my fellow suffragettes and I traveled around this country. We marched and held signs until change came. New York was one of the last places I paraded for women's votes."

The train halted, and a man in uniform placed a stool below steps leading up into the train car. He assisted them up the stairs. After asking for their destination, the conductor directed them to a car on the left. From there, they found a pair of seats facing a dozing woman and child.

As they settled in their chairs, Betsy thought back on what Miss Woodson said about participating in the marches. "It must have been exciting to travel so many places, but how did you support yourself?"

Miss Woodson smoothed her skirts before answering. "I was lucky enough to have parents who ran a newspaper. My traveling away from home brought on a few arguments from Father, but Mother supported women's rights. She worked for allowing all people to vote for most of her adult life. She convinced Father my travels would serve two purposes. I could continue my work as a reporter for the paper and also support the cause. At first, Father was hesitant to send me so far from home. He said he'd seen too much of the bad side of humankind during the War Between the States and was concerned for my safety."

"Someone told me the marches became violent at times." The train car lurched forward. Betsy gripped her armrest and watched the depot appear to slide away as Miss Woodson cleared her throat.

"We faced some trouble." She sighed and touched a small scar on her cheek. "I did see the bad side of a few people who taunted us and threw rocks when we marched into Washington, DC, back in 1913. Unfortunately, I also saw some women who brought trouble to themselves and the rest of the group. I chose not to be part of the group trying to win the vote with violence during the following years. Instead, I chose to fight through the written word. I even talked Father into carrying Kewpie Doll Cartoons in our paper. Rose O'Neill, who drew the Kewpies, openly asked for the women's votes through her cute little cupid-like comics."

"I played with Kewpie Kut-Out paper dolls at one time. I didn't realize they were part of getting the vote." A splash of childhood memories made Betsy recall a sweet moment when she and her mother played with the toy. Her hard-working mother hadn't mentioned anything political during their fun.

Miss Woodson cleared her throat. "There were many ways to fight for our rights. Rose O'Neill fought using art while others used music and words."

"Thank you for helping get women the vote. You served us all well. For the sake of single women like June, Margie, and me, I pray women will be able to keep or find jobs now."

"Mrs. Roosevelt's speech to the United Nations back in February should help ladies all around the world. The war showed men how women could keep the workplace running while they were away at war. The same thing happened during the first world war. Mother served our paper by herself during the Civil War. She wasn't even married to Father at the time."

"I feel a little guilty for not helping out as much as June and Margie." Betsy watched trees blur as the train flew down the tracks.

"There is no reason for those feelings." Miss Woodson patted her hand. "Your work for me was important in many ways. You helped me write articles for the paper when the men I hired as reporters went to war. The errands you ran for me allowed the paper to survive. You served as the messenger between me and the people who have run the paper since my retirement. It took all of us to get through this conflict and the Great Depression we survived in the previous years."

"I was glad to help you. I enjoyed helping write stories for the paper."

"Your sacrifice brought us to this point. I would have lost Woodson House if it hadn't been for your willingness to work for room and board, instead of pay, during the worst of times. I just hope our young men don't have to deal with as many issues as my father did when he came home without a leg. It took him a long time to accept Mother's love and to overcome all he had endured." Miss Woodson looked out the train window. A wistful expression crossed her face.

"My brother and I were born very late in their lives due to him trying to avoid marriage and the love Mother offered. She was in her late thirties when he proposed. Early in their marriage, they lost several children. Eventually my brother Warren was born. I arrived about ten months later. The war and my father's first wife's death did terrible things to his mind. He still struggled throughout his entire life, but Mother helped him to the best of her ability."

Betsy nodded. "I think both Paul and Dale fared well during the war. Neither saw much danger during the times they served. Paul's child won't be an old-age blessing since they are already expecting. Dale seems content to continue his work at the factory while he tries to figure out what his mother wanted him to find."

"I'm glad you've gotten to know Dale better. He seems like a nice man, one worthy of your affection, should you choose to give him the time of day." A mischievous grin spread across the older woman's face.

Betsy crossed her arms. "I want my chance to live in the city for a while before I consider settling down. You experienced your days of traveling and seem to have done well without marrying."

Miss Woodson looked at the sleeping child across from them. Her chest heaved. "There were some things I never experienced — things I will regret when I'm older and have to rely more on help from others."

"I'm sorry." Betsy gave the woman's hand a squeeze.

"There's nothing for you to be sorry about. I made choices limiting what I did with my years so far. Give yourself a chance to experience all life and love has to offer. You might find a change in plans may be what God wants for you." She leaned back in the seat and wiped a handkerchief across her sweat-covered brow as a silence fell between them.

Ginny

Present day

Ginny never thought they'd be working on the paperwork for foster care. She struggled to put the words into the form that would change all their plans. Her impression of the institution pushed doubts into her mind about whether she could handle the temporary relationship. Fostering would most likely end in a parting, a saying goodbye. The Russell family and Melissa were fresh reminders of what could happen. She looked at Scott. His expression appeared to be asking her a question of his own. His hands were open on his lap.

She rose and paced the room. "Do you think we're making the right decision to take on a foster child? We both decided to step back from the busyness of our lives since we lost Violet."

He blocked her path and wrapped his arms around her, leaning his forehead against hers. "I will abide by your wishes, but I think we've both given our hearts to Melissa. She isn't going to be a stranger. We know her situation and what could happen. From what I saw during the play, she may be what our hearts need right now, someone to love, even if the relationship is not permanent. I can tell she loves you."

She stepped out of his arms. "But what if she loves us too much and then is forced to leave? Right now, she's dealing with parting from the Russells." Ginny placed a hand on her forehead and turned away.

Scott rubbed her back. "Then maybe we need to let her go and leave her future in God's hands. We should pray about this and give ourselves a few days before we make a final decision." He held her closer as she listened to his prayer. "Help us to know Your will, Father. We're confused right now and lay this burden at Your feet. May blessings flow to Melissa. She is a dear child to You and to us. We don't want to do anything to hurt her. Please comfort us as we mourn the passing of Violet. She is in Your tender hands. May Your will be done. In Jesus' name we pray, amen."

Even before his final amen, Ginny knew what needed to be done. They sat in silence for a few moments, then she squeezed his hand. "Since we've laid it at God's feet, I feel much better about the situation." She bent her head back and smiled up at Scott. "How about you, are you ready to be a foster dad?"

"I am." He covered her mouth with a sweet kiss. They rocked from side-to-side in a sweet dance of love and hope.

Chapter Eighteen

Betsy
1946

Speeding down the tracks, the train swayed from side-to-side, with an occasional jolt rattling the car. Betsy's lack of sleep from the night before and the rocking motion soon sent her into a restless slumber. Her head drooped to the side. The cool windowpane relieved some of the warmth in the compartment. Sometime during her on-and-off dozing, she sensed Miss Woodson had pulled out her old-fashioned fan. The fluttering resulted in a sandalwood-scented breeze refreshing the other half of Betsy's face. Dreams of city life swirled and twisted with visions of Dale standing in front of Woodson House wearing a straw hat and holding a pitchfork. The occasional interruption of the conductor's sing-song voice calling out cities as the train slowed to a stop barely registered. Neither did the lurch forward after new passengers found seating in their passenger car. Then the smell of bread and cold fried chicken filtered into her nose, making her stomach rumble. She forced her eyes open.

"Did you have a good rest?" The open basket Margie packed for their trip rested on Miss Woodson's lap. She held out a piece of chicken wrapped in waxed paper.

"I tried to catch a nap, but it wasn't as nice as sleeping on my bed at Woodson House." Betsy rubbed her eyes and took the piece of chicken from her employer. She inhaled the welcome aroma before taking a bite. Rumbles made their way from her midsection. "This tastes wonderful. I'm starved."

Apples and biscuits rounded out their meal as the train slowed and shifted to a side-track outside of a station. The train shuddered and thumped. Betsy jumped and almost choked on her food.

The conductor ambled through the car, holding onto seatbacks. "We're switching engines, folks. No need to worry. Half our cars are bound for New York, the other half for places to the south. From here on, a diesel engine will pull us to the big city."

Another jolt shook the car and the echoing effect of other cars accepting the new engine rattled down the track in succession.

Betsy leaned over Miss Woodson and waved to the conductor. "How much farther until we get to New York?"

"It will be several hours, Miss, but the engine we have now should pull us along at a good clip. There aren't as many towns here in the

Pennsylvania woods, so we won't stop as often during the rest of your trip." He tapped his dark cap in a two-finger salute and moved down the aisle.

Miss Woodson dusted crumbs from her lap and wiped her hands on a handkerchief. She reached into a side pocket of her bag and pulled out her knitting needles. Pastel green yarn wrapped and twisted around the pointed tools, under control of her deft fingers, until the shape of a baby bootie began to form. "We can't have Paul and Ellen's child having cold feet after the little one is born."

Betsy pulled out the envelope containing the last few poems from the packet Miss Woodson gave her. Maybe reading one of them aloud would help pass the time. She scanned both pieces of paper. Folding one of them back into the wrapper, she smiled as she read to the rhythm of Miss Woodson's clacking needles.

Birthday

Today another child was born.
I'm happy though my body's worn.
The doctor says there'll be no more,
This babe's the last God has in store.

My Sam says two will fill his breast,
With hope and peace, that we are blessed.
My little one lays snuggled near,
Big brother holds her hand, so dear.

My husband's lips touch mine in love,
Our family's whole, thank God above.
We have a daughter and a boy.
Our lives are blessed with love and joy.

I'll fill the halls of Woodson House,
With these two children and my spouse.
The years we lost, are lost no more.
The future's now an open door.

I'll take a break from outside life
Accept the role of loving wife.
We lived a lifetime steeped in woe
But now it's past, our love can grow.

These children sitting here with me,
Will know we fought to make men free.

But we will raise them in God's care,
And hope they see the love we share.

The legacy of this old place,
Is mine to share, to love, embrace.
It served my aunts and runaways,
Now it will be a place of grace.

I thank the Lord for answered prayer,
For all the years which we will share,
With children who will make my heart,
A place where they will not depart.

Miss Woodson's clicking needles stilled as she pulled them closer to her chest. "My mother may be long gone, but her memory still lives in my heart. No one can take those sweet moments away from me. Thank you for sharing the precious reminder."

Betsy laid her palm over her friend's fisted fingers. "My mother lives in my heart too. I don't look forward to the day when she is gone."

"But whose heart do I live in?" A tear trickled down Miss Woodson's wrinkled cheek.

"You've been like an adopted mother to all of your boarders and your niece Lottie's family. You will stay in our hearts forever, whether you like it or not." Betsy leaned closer to the woman and then drew back. "Ouch, those knitting needles may keep some of us at a distance."

They both laughed and began watching the scenery outside the speeding train's windows. Many hours later, trees gave way to neighborhoods and then tall city buildings, which faded as they dipped into a dark tunnel taking their train into New York City's Grand Central Station.

Ginny
Present day

The next morning, Chelsea Russell brought Melissa into the classroom a few minutes early. Dark puffy areas were noticeable beneath the girl's eyes. She wore a forced smile as she handed in papers from her missed day and hugged her foster mom goodbye.

Ginny greeted them, and lightly touched the girl's shoulder. She whispered, "I'm praying for you."

The words seemed to encourage Melissa. Her slumped shoulders straightened. "Thank you, Miss Cline. I'm going to do my best today, so you will be very proud of me."

Ginny didn't correct the child's use of her maiden name. She gave her a side hug. "I'm always proud of you. You are a strong young lady. I don't know if I ever told you about another strong young woman named Melissa. I've been reading her poems. She's taught me a lot about being courageous."

"Another Melissa, I never heard of someone who has the same name. I don't remember you telling me anything about her." The child's eyes begged for more information.

"Her given name was Melissa, but she went by the name of Missy. She was a real-life person who inspired the character of Christine in the musical I wrote."

"I remember her. She was the nice lady who helped the person I acted escape to freedom at Woodson House. You got to be her during the last night of the musical. She reminded me of you in real life."

Melissa's chatter touched Ginny's heart. She swallowed a lump in her throat. It was good to hear the youngster sounding more like her normal self. A sliver of hope trilled its way across Ginny's chest. Last night, she and Scott agreed to submit both foster and adoption papers. He'd promised to drop both forms at Children's Services this morning on his way to campus.

Hopefully, the paperwork would get priority and they'd be able to help Melissa if things didn't work out with her birthmother. Ginny hated to admit she hoped the mother would not get custody. She knew too much about the woman's past relationship with her daughter. People could change, but up to this point Melissa's parent had made little progress.

As other students entered the classroom, Ginny rose to greet them. Melissa sat down in her usual seat. She chatted with her classmates until the day officially began with pledges and morning announcements. Several children cheered at the mention of a talent show.

"Maybe we can sing one of the songs Miss Cline wrote. Oops, I mean Mrs. Hallmark." Melissa's suggestion set the class into a flurry of conversation about talents. Two students, who recently moved to town, did not believe their teacher wrote music.

Ginny laughed at their disbelief as she pulled up a file onto her computer, from *Incident at Woodson House*. She turned on the classroom's interactive screen and projector, and then pressed *play*. The students grew quiet as Melissa and Ginny's friend, Hope, stepped into the spotlight and sang.

"Hey, I recognize Melissa in a dirty dress, and I know the other lady. My mom buys craft stuff from Miss Hope's fabric store." Someone shushed the commenter. The rest of the class listened in admiration.

"Wow, you did good, Melissa." One of the boys who sat near the girl looked at the video in amazement.

"Thanks." Melissa's grin spread wider than Ginny had ever noticed before.

"Could we sing the song for the talent show?" Melissa's friend Joy begged.

About half the class cheered.

"It was pretty, but it sounded too sad. Do you have a happier song, Mrs. Hallmark?" Another student voiced her opinion and several others nodded their agreement.

A whole room of hopeful faces turned toward their teacher after the student's observation.

Ginny felt giddy. The pull to create something new tickled its way down to her fingers. "Give me a day or two and I'll see what I can come up with. In the meantime, what are some ideas you'd like to see in a song?" She opened a blank page on her projected computer screen and wrote down their suggestions.

Several ideas centered on friendship, so she asked the children to write a short story about the topic using their best writing skills, then turn it in for their Language Arts assignment. It met the standard for the day's lesson. She'd just changed the prompt to their current interests.

While the students were at physical education, she read through their work. The words forming in her head might become the children's requested song.

1. Sometimes days are much too rough,
Life gets tumbled, tossed, and tough.
But friends who show they truly care,
Will help you with the loads you bear. So...

(Chorus) Make a friend, reach for a hand
Work together, take a stand.
Show concern to those in need
Demonstrate through love and deed.

2. Look around to see who's sad,
Feeling lost, or really mad.
Let them know they have a friend
They can count on to the end. So...
(Chorus)

Two verses and a chorus would get the piece started. Ginny decided the children should help with the rest of the stanzas. Their contribution would ensure they owned most of the song. She wanted to share the glory with her students and not take it all for herself. She'd overcome her bitterness about James stealing her college musical for his own work. Maybe she should have encouraged him to help create some of the play from so long ago, instead of trying to do the work herself.

Perhaps the temptation wouldn't have been so great for him to take the whole thing if he'd been more involved. She felt relief knowing they'd reached a point of forgiveness. She was glad their college interest in each other hadn't worked out. Scott sated her heart with emotions she'd never experienced with James during college. Besides, Melody seemed somewhat interested in the man. Maybe someday a love interest would grow between those two.

Ginny typed the words into her computer and projected them onto the screen for the children to see when they returned. There were a few more minutes before the students finished gym, so she read several more of their papers. Their ideas were great and easily transferable into the song. She used phrases from the few papers she'd read as examples for building another verse for their creation. She looked at the clock and realized she needed to retrieve her students from their activity. Then they could use the next hour to work on putting their words to the melody.

Scott
Present day

Scott stood in the back of the packed auditorium watching Ginny's class sing their talent show song. His eyes focused on the young girl who would be heading to their home the following day. Her smile and enthusiasm added depth to the lyrics and melody. In his opinion, her performance sparkled. The child had touched his heart during last year's summer drama camp and during her role in the musical.

After going through a couple of hectic weeks of online training, he and Ginny received approval as Melissa's foster parents. The fact they were both teachers and the Russell family move was imminent helped to ease the transition, according to their case worker. So much for trying to cut back on activities, but in the long run, he knew they were doing right. He and Ginny were both happier in the last few days.

Tomorrow was the May Election Day. Students had the day off. Teachers were supposed to work on class lists for next year. Ginny told him the administration informed the faculty to plan those lists two ways. One would reflect the passage of a school levy. The other list would show higher numbers in each classroom due to cuts. He knew his wife had provided Kara, her fellow fourth-grade teacher, with a list of suggestions for next year's groupings. Scott was glad Ginny had opted to take a family leave day tomorrow to welcome Melissa into their home.

~~~~~
~~~~~

Early the next morning, Scott wrapped his arms around his wife as she tossed and turned in their bed. "I love you, sweetheart. Are you ready to add to our family this afternoon?"

"I love you too. I'm so excited, I hardly slept."

"I noticed. You're going to be a wonderful foster mom. You have nothing to worry about." He pulled her closer for a kiss.

Once the sun rose, he slid from beneath the covers. Ginny sighed and hugged his pillow close. Sleep finally claimed her. He brushed his lips across hers and left her dreaming. He headed to the kitchen with the dogs trotting beside him. After he released them to the backyard, he ate one of the muffins Ginny baked during the weekend. She'd spent most of Sunday afternoon preparing treats to offer their foster daughter when she arrived. His stomach hadn't complained when she'd mentioned there were plenty of muffins for breakfast.

The dogs barked and he let them in, hoping they didn't wake Ginny. Willing pups vacuumed crumbs from the floor with their tongues, and then trotted off to find sunny spots near windows. Scott hoped Melissa was going to enjoy having pets.

Grabbing his bag, he headed for the door. He would attend an early class taking their final exam and then return in time for Melissa's arrival. Ginny and he both voted absentee, so they had nothing else on their day's agenda. Warm breezes blessed the spring day. It was almost a year since he walked into the local elementary school and literally ran into Ginny. So many things had happened since then.

~~~~~

Two hours later, his last student turned in her test.

"Have a great summer vacation," he said.

"You too, Professor Hallmark. By the way, I registered to be an intern for the arts department next year. There should be a request for a reference in your email."

"Thanks, I'll check it out. I'm sure you will do a fantastic job if you get the position." Scott waved to the departing student and opened his email on the classroom computer. Sure enough, the reference request was near the top, beneath an email from his direct supervisor, Amber Whitney, who was also the department chair. The subject line read 'tenure track status.'

Scott pressed his palms together and whispered a prayer of hope or in the worst case, acceptance of what might come. Releasing his hands, he clicked on the message. It was brief:

Congratulations. You are now on the tenure track. By the way, I am stepping aside as department chair. I want to devote more time to opening my retail studio. No one else is interested in chairing at this point. The job can be yours for the asking. The dean said it doesn't
~~~~~

matter if you are fairly new to the department.

The words lifted a load of baggage from his shoulders. His journey towards becoming tenured had begun. The extra pay for being a department chair would go far with their future financial status in question. He grabbed his bag of final exams and headed home to welcome Melissa. He could hardly wait to tell his wife and foster daughter the news about his new status.

Chapter Nineteen

Betsy
1946

Red-capped men waited near the baggage car, ready to assist riders with their luggage. Betsy handed Miss Woodson their satchels and took both suitcases from the cart full of offloaded baggage. Her employer warned her, before they stepped from the train, about the men expecting payment for their services. Betsy needed to be frugal, starting with managing their luggage.

She was breathing hard by the time they arrived inside the main terminal. Her head swiveled in awe as she stared at the vaulted ceilings decorated with ornate designs. Then she laughed. They'd used acorns, simple country seeds, as part of the artistic embellishments. Maybe the city folk longed for the country.

Miss Woodson stepped ahead of Betsy and led her outside. They made their way down sidewalks bustling with humanity. "It isn't too far to their apartment from here. We'll walk down 42nd until we get to Bryant Park. My grand-nephew, Woody Franklin, and his wife, Maxine, live near there."

Betsy glanced up at the tall buildings as they wove through crowds of people heading toward the train station or moving toward skyscraper homes. She forced her focus to the earth after bumping into several rushing people. When they came to the park, she stared in awe at the majestic lion statues positioned near the steps to the huge library. Discovering the books in the building would be an adventure and it wouldn't cost anything.

They paused a moment to study the marble monument and statue of William Cullen Bryant. Betsy set down the bags and shook out her wrists. She tried to focus on Miss Woodson's words about the poet. She held in a laugh as several cooing pigeons left their mark on the image's bronze shoulders.

"Are you listening, dear?" The older woman pointed to the sculpture without smiling. "My mother always appreciated the man's poetry. He was quite famous in his day and wrote a few abolitionist pieces. He was a newspaperman, like my father."

Miss Woodson turned away and led them across the park until they reached a splashing fountain in the middle of a circular pool. "Take note of this memorial. It is dedicated to a woman, which you don't find too often these days. Maybe things will change since we finished another war where the women played a vital role. Josephine Shaw Lowell worked to help the poor find a better life. She was the first woman to serve on the board for charities here in New York. She wanted women treated with respect in the workplace. Her thoughts remind me of one of my mother's works. Mom made me memorize the poem. Let me see if I still recall the piece."

Good News

This week's headline brings good news.
Shows the world has changed its views.
When it comes to women's voting,
All must see these words worth noting.

Not the last step, but a gain,
Fills my mind in sweet refrain.
Western women have new rights.
Let us hope their spark ignites.

May a flame spread through this land,
Warming hearts to take a stand,
For the suffrage, we've endured,
'Til our voting is ensured.

"Ladies in the west got the vote before the whole nation. It took a while for everyone to agree. There are still many rights women need to gain for themselves."

"Those words sound like what Margie has been talking about. She'd enjoy seeing this fountain and the library." Betsy picked up the suitcases and hurried behind Miss Woodson as she stepped from the elevated area and headed down a nearby side street.

A few moments, later they stopped in a vestibule, waiting for an elevator. The doors slid open and they entered the wood-paneled car. A young redheaded woman wearing a double-breasted uniform ushered them into the elevator. She closed the wooden doors, then pulled a clanking metal gate into place.

"Hello, my name is Ruby. Where would you like to go?"

"Please take us to the fifth floor. We are visiting some of my family." Miss Woodson smiled at Ruby.

"I heard Mr. and Mrs. Woodson Franklin were having visitors. Welcome to New York City." The young woman stepped to the left of the cabin, pulled at a knob on a circular controller, and swiveled it to the left.

Betsy grabbed onto the bronze railing and watched the floors pass by in front of the metal gate. When the number five appeared, the operator slowed the ascent and the car bounced a few times as the girl tried to line up with the line indicating a floor.

"Sorry, I've only worked here for a few weeks." She opened the gate and pulled wooden doors to the side. She tipped her hat to them.

"You did fine. I hope you have a nice day." Miss Woodson dropped a coin into the hat, and they made their way down a stuffy hallway to apartment fifty-five.

After a quick rap on the door, it opened to reveal a dark-haired woman, who welcomed them into their home away from home. She brushed a kiss across Miss Woodson's weathered cheek. "Welcome Auntie and Betsy."

She led them down a thin hallway and directed the visitors into a room on the right. The bedroom they would share wasn't much larger than Betsy's small space back at Woodson House. They managed to squeeze in beside the bed and lay their suitcases on top of an oak dresser.

"I hope you will enjoy the city this week. We love the hustle and bustle. Woody will be home from work soon, and then we can have a bite to eat. By the way, I'm Maxine." With their hands free, the middle-aged woman reached out and shook Betsy's hand.

A hint of something roasting in an oven wafted through the apartment. Betsy's mouth watered. Thoughts of a warm dinner distracted her until she heard her name.

"Betsy wants to see what it's like to live and work in the city while we visit." Miss Woodson gave her grand-niece-in-law a hug as she chattered on about seeing the Statue of Liberty, library, and Chrysler Building. "Did Woody get a chance to see if Betsy could go to work with him one day?"

"Actually, his secretary is off for a doctor's appointment on Thursday. I heard about your great clerical skills, so you can experience the life of a city business first-hand. I usually go into work when someone is out of the office, but this will give me more time to catch up with Auntie."

Maxine led them back into her living room, which also contained a dining table. A rotating fan sat near an open window. It brought in a breeze laden with exhaust fumes, as it distorted the sound of honking horns on the streets below.

Betsy's nose itched. A slight throb thudded in her temples. The trip must be catching up with her. "Could I make use of the powder room?"

"Of course, where are my manners? Our restroom is the first door to the left in the hallway. You'll find it right before the room you are staying in. I'll prepare some tea while you freshen up. There are washcloths under the sink if you want to wash your face."

"Thank you." Betsy rose from the chair and made her way to the tiny room. After using the facilities, she splashed her face and felt a little relief. Cupping her hand, she lifted water into her mouth. The taste of the tepid liquid didn't resemble anything she'd tasted before. Instead of swallowing, she swished it around in her mouth and spat it out. She hoped Maxine's tea would cover the taste with something more pleasant.

Betsy looked into the small mirror and finger-combed her hair back into a low bun. She twisted the glass doorknob and exited the marble-tiled room. The carpet runner in the narrow hallway muffled her footsteps. Cheerful voices greeted her when she walked back into the living area.

"These are so sweet. I've never used a tea strainer or infuser resembling a tiny teapot." Miss Woodson held the chain and dipped the shiny metal item up and down in her china teacup.

"They were a family heirloom, recently given to me by my mother. Tiffany's, a well-known jeweler here in town, created them out of pure silver. I put a little mint in with the tea leaves. I hope you don't mind."

"The mint sounds perfect." Betsy held the cup close to her nose and inhaled as the water began to take on a darker amber hue. She could see a hint of light coming through the upper part of the cup where the liquid didn't reach. "Your china is beautiful too."

"This setting was a wedding gift. I love the delicate flowers. The pattern was one of the Haviland Company's more popular choices when we were married. You'll have a chance to see the plates for the evening meal."

"So, how did you meet Miss Woodson's grand-nephew?" Betsy savored a sip of tea. The fragrance and liquid were a welcome respite from her travels. She took a longer drink and felt better as she waited for Maxine's answer.

"My father hired him to work in our office. I went to secretarial school. My parents thought I'd get a good start working in the family business. Woody came to New York for his education and applied to work in our office. A few months after he was hired, my parents started hinting he might be a good man to become a permanent part of the business, and family. I heartily agreed, since he was so sweet. Not long after we started going together, we set a date for our wedding. How about you? Is there anyone in your future?"

Betsy strangled on the half-swallowed tea in her throat. Warmth covered her cheeks by the time she took another sip and settled down enough to answer in a croaking voice. "I want to give life in the city a try, before I settle down with anyone."

Miss Woodson giggled. "We do have a very eligible man at the boarding house right now. I don't think it would take much on Betsy's part to encourage a romance."

"Dale has other things on his mind besides romance." Betsy took another swallow and cleared her throat.

"Dale? So you're on a first-name basis with the man?"

A rattle of keys at the door saved Betsy from answering Maxine's query. Woody entered the apartment and settled his hat on a rack near the door. "Auntie, it's so good to see you."

Miss Woodson stood, and he wrapped his arms around her.

After Miss Woodson introduced Betsy, the younger woman helped Maxine set the table and bring out roast beef, carrots, and potatoes from the side room, serving as a kitchen. The small roasting pan barely fit inside the oven when Maxine tugged it out for Betsy to transfer the food into serving dishes. When all was ready, they took their places around a table built for four, the perfect size for the apartment, and joined hands. The food smelled heavenly as they bowed their heads and gave thanks.

Dale
1946

Dale bowed his head for a moment and offered a brief prayer for the restaurant meal he'd ordered. He poked at the chicken. It didn't seem quite done, but he didn't want to complain. At least it got him out of the house. Ever since Betsy and Miss Woodson took off for the city, he'd felt a little awkward. The other women at the boarding house were fine cooks. But he felt out of place having June batting her eyes at him, without Betsy in the room to provide a little space.

Margie didn't stare, but she wanted to fuss about women getting equal pay at work. He didn't mind the idea. He just didn't want to argue with her when she thought he was against it. He told her he thought it was a fine idea, but then she wanted him to stand up for women and do something about it. He poked a fork into a stiff green bean. His ma always cooked them until they were soft. Crunching down on it, he decided to make do with what the restaurant served.

Dale needed to load up his belly to avoid being discovered looking for a snack later in the night. June seemed to know when he was in the kitchen and came in all ready to help. At least the restaurant knew how to make mashed potatoes and gravy. He cleaned his plate by adding a spoonful of potatoes to each bite of the other food.

"Would you like dessert? We have a choice between apple and cherry pies with a dab of whipped cream." A young woman wearing an apron over her peach-colored dress held her pencil poised over an order pad.

"I'd love a slice of cherry pie if you can change the order to a heap of whipped cream instead of a dab."

"Sure thing, Mister. I'll have your order out in a minute." She grabbed his empty plate and headed for the kitchen. "One cherry pie, heavy on the cream."

He watched out the window, both seeing and hearing the train chugging into town for the nightly delivery. He'd have plenty to do tomorrow at work if they managed to send the correct orders this time. There were still a few shortages in the aftermath of the war. At least he had a job for a while. The chemist position was something to be thankful for in the changing world.

"Here you go, sir. Can I get you another cup of coffee?" The waitress set down the pie and a fresh fork.

"I'm good, thank you. Have a nice day." He nodded and glanced her way.

"You, too." Her smile reminded him too much of June's. He turned away from her gaze and focused on the warm piece of pie and melting cream. The satisfying sweetness in his mouth made up for the rest of the meal. He left some coins on the table and walked to the counter to pay his bill. The older man, who rang up the sale, reminded him of his step-pa. Papa Herbert had proved himself as a good father to Dale, for most of their lives. Too bad the war had messed with their family.

Ginny
Present day

Ginny opened her door to Loretta. The woman gave her a brief squeeze and then breezed forward like a soldier ready for war. Her bright floral top billowed out behind her like a sail. She hurried into the formal dining area where several women set up shop around the plastic-covered table. Lilac scented the room as she presented her weapons of war, a pack of small pots for planting, and a stack of cards bearing the picture of an angel among violets.

Melissa reached for a card and held it up. "These are beautiful, Miss Loretta. Mama Ginny said you painted the picture yourself."

"She sure did." Honey gave the newcomer a welcoming hug. "Thanks for sharing your talent, dear. Now let's get down to business. Ginny has this wonderful idea, and we are going to make it a reality. Who wants to be on our distribution committee? Annabelle has offered to help from home when her husband's health allows. Annie said we could put out flyers at the Historical Museum."

Ginny watched from her seat as Honey and Loretta organized the other ladies into distributers, card signers, and violet growers. Several women brought cups of leaves taken from violet plants. Honey's contribution was a large bag of African violet potting soil and several blossoming plants. Organized chaos ensued as the ladies began working on their tasks. In the distance, howling resounded from Ginny's laundry room, where Jezebel and Carlos made their voices heard above the feminine chatter.

Melissa leaned into Ginny's side, her voice barely audible above the din. "My mom lost several babies. I might have been part of a bigger family. Some of them I helped Ma to de--…" She swiped at her eyes as the women around them grew quiet. "Do you think we could send her a card and flower?"

Ginny hugged the girl close. Sorrow for what the young girl might have seen and gone through shredded her soul. "I'm sorry, sweetheart. We'll make sure she gets one."

Honey hovered over them, surrounding them with her arms. "You and your mother will each get a flower of your own. Though we'd like to give your Mama Ginny our first official card and flower." She presented Ginny and Melissa with fully grown plants. The ruffled lavender-hued flowers sparkled with their tears. Every woman in the group signed the cards presented to them.

"I guess I'm pretty lucky to have two mamas in my family." Melissa leaned closer to her foster mother. Warm feelings flowed as Ginny absorbed the child's love.

"Don't forget, you now have a whole room full of grandmothers who love you with all our hearts too. Don't you agree, ladies?" Loretta's open arms surrounded Ginny and Melissa in a lilac cloud. Ginny held back a laugh as her foster daughter squirmed out of the hug and escaped to check on the dogs.

Chapter Twenty

Betsy
1946

After Betsy's return from the city, the Woodson House seemed to welcome her with open arms. The relatively quiet neighborhood full of chirping birds and only an occasional sound from a passing car seemed like home. It wasn't the noisy city she once yearned for, nor was it the country where she'd been raised. Though, if she had to choose, she now saw the benefits of country life as more advantageous than what she'd seen in the city. As she hefted their suitcases up the front porch steps, she smiled at her employer.

"Thank you for taking me to the city, Miss Woodson. It was an adventure, but I think I'd rather stay here and work for you."

"I hoped you'd see it my way. I've grown to admire you and appreciate what you do for me. However, if a certain young man steals you away, you have my blessings." The older woman chuckled and winked as Betsy set their bags inside and held the door wide open for her.

Heat rose under Betsy's collar. It was a good thing the entry light wasn't on for the rest of the world to see her feelings written all over her face. She shook her head and took Miss Woodson's bag into the woman's quarters before hurrying to take her own luggage up the stairs.

As she ran up the steps, she heard Miss Woodson giggle. Betsy felt the sudden urge to get a soapy rag and wash away the dirt and memories of the city, along with the pink stains covering her cheeks.

"Are you all right?"

Just what she needed... Dale peered down from the top of the stairs. She must look a sight with her flaming face.

"Let me help you with your suitcase. It looks like you could use a little aid." He reached out and easily lifted her case up the rest of the steps. His own complexion colored as he paused before her door and set the bag down without entering her room. He cleared his throat. "Did you have a good time?"

"It was an eye-opening experience. I enjoyed seeing the sights and meeting more of the Woodson family. New York was such a busy place. It's good to be back home."

"I'm glad you're here. The boarding house seemed a little lonesome without you." Dale looked at his shoes and then looked directly at her.

A glimmer of something sparked between them. Betsy couldn't

contain the smile bubbling up from deep within.

Dale matched her look with one of his own. "I hope you don't mind but I brought you a little gift. I'll be right back." He hurried into his room, returning with something behind his back. "My supervisor's wife raises these plants. He brought in several to share and I thought of you. It's called an African Violet. Apparently, you can grow a new one with just a single leaf." He pulled a small pot holding velvety leaves and purple blossoms.

Betsy accepted the gift and ran her finger over the soft leaves. "I always wanted one of these plants. Your gift is an answer to one of my fondest dreams." She struggled with something else to say but only managed to blurt out, "Thank you, Dale."

"You're welcome. While you were away, I discovered a restaurant. They make great desserts. Would you be interested in maybe..."

"I'd love to eat out with you sometime." A wave of giddiness welled up in her chest. She'd resisted him, but the time seemed right for their relationship to change.

He chuckled. His shoulders visibly relaxed. "I can't speak well of the meals, but I'd love to take you there for an after-dinner treat sometime."

June and Margie's chatter reached their ears as the two women's shoes could be heard pounding up the stairs. The couple stepped to their separate doorways and waved before shutting themselves into their own rooms. Betsy leaned against the inside of her door. She placed a hand on her chest and sighed.

After setting the plant on the old desk, a knock on her door broke into her thoughts.

"Hey, Betsy, are you in there? If you are, can you move your suitcase out of the middle of the hallway?" June's voice trumpeted from just outside the door.

"Once this luggage is stowed away, we want to hear all about the trip to New York City." Margie's calmer voice held genuine interest in the New York visit.

Betsy composed herself and opened her door. She toted her suitcase into the room, set it on her bed, and opened it up. Her friends crowded in and found seats in the small room. Their expressions were hopeful as she gathered her thoughts.

"The city was huge. Margie might enjoy the gigantic library, not far from the Woodson's apartment."

"Tell me more. I'd love to work in a city library someday." Margie's face glowed with excitement. She leaned forward from her perch on the side of the bed.

"I've never seen so many bookshelves. If I had the time or a library card, I'm sure I could have read every single day." Thinking of all the books lightened Betsy's thoughts. "They even owned an extensive collection of Grace Livingston Hill novels." She removed her copy of *Lo, Michael* from her suitcase and placed it on her pillow. She was almost finished with the story, again.

"I wouldn't use my time reading books if I was in a city teeming with handsome businessmen." June sat at the old desk, planted her elbow, and rested her chin on her palm. Her arched eyebrows urged Betsy to share more.

"I'm afraid most of them wouldn't even notice you. The fellows I saw tended to be in a hurry as they marched on crowded sidewalks. The sounds overwhelmed me when busy streets clogged up with all kinds of people rushing to unknown destinations." Thoughts of shadowed sidewalks and people pushing their way past clouded Betsy's memories.

"It sounds like fun to me." June leaned back in the desk chair, almost falling backward.

"The noise in the city kept me from sleeping most nights. It was much hotter there, so we left the windows open. Fumes and noises from motorized vehicles poured in around the clock." Betsy wrinkled her nose as she thought about the smells.

"Did the Woodson relatives take you out for an automobile ride?" Margie rubbed her hands together.

Betsy shook her head. "They went everywhere on foot or took the bus. Mr. Woodson Franklin's office was only several blocks away, so we walked there. I worked a day in his office, but I got confused when everything needed to be done faster than I could think." She lifted one of her new dresses from her suitcase and held it up for the others to admire. "I did come home with a couple of nice things."

June ran her finger down the stylish dress. "This outfit sure is pretty. If you ever want to share, I'd be glad to borrow it."

Margie snickered. "You two aren't exactly the same size."

Betsy joined the laughter as she reached into a side pocket of her suitcase and pulled out the packet of postcards she'd purchased. "I'm glad I traveled there and saw some famous buildings and monuments, but it is wonderful to be home." She opened the accordion-folded strip of cards and held them up for the other young women to peruse.

Margie leaned in closer and pointed to one of the cards. "My mother talked about seeing the Statue of Liberty when she immigrated here after the First World War. She met my father when he served overseas during the conflict. She was his nurse in a British hospital after he suffered an injury. Once her duties as a military medic were over, she came to the United States and they married."

"How romantic." June pretended to swoon, and this time the desk chair pitched her to the floor. The other two came to her rescue. All three burst into gales of laughter.

Dale
1946

Dale heard the giggles pealing down the hallway of the old home. Doubt engulfed him as he wondered if they were laughing at his gift, or his desire to take Betsy out on a date. He dropped onto the side of the bed and lifted his eyes toward the ceiling. *Help me, Lord. Have I messed up by asking her out? I pray they are cackling about something besides me or my attempt at a gift.* Maybe his nerves were getting to him. He'd been avoiding a relationship for so long.

Their laughter probably had no relation to his gift or to his offer for a date. He stretched out on the bed and put his hands behind his head. She'd said yes to going out. Surely her hopeful expression meant something when he mentioned dating. The way she'd accepted his gift and held it close spoke volumes. He closed his eyes and envisioned Betsy's smile when she saw the flower. He hoped it lived. He knew all about growing corn and beans. His mother taught him how to take care of her outdoor flowers around the farmhouse, but indoor plants were another matter.

Ring, ring, ring. Three rings meant a call was coming in for the Woodson House. Two rings were for another home on their party line. June admitted she sometimes listened in on the other line to hear gossiping cousins. Gossiping was another strike against the good-looking woman. Her personality tended to grind against his being, like a rough piece of sandpaper.

"Dale, it's for you." Miss Woodson's normally quiet voice echoed up the stairway. A sense of foreboding brought Dale to his feet. His door bounced off the wall as he bounded down the stairs and took the receiver from his landlord.

"The call is from your mother." The older woman's hands shook as she wrung them together.

Dale nodded his thanks. The wire between the rotary phone and handset only stretched so far. He sat down. "Hello, Ma, is everything all right?"

The line crackled as Ma spoke, but he was able to make out her words. "We just got back from the hospital. Herbert broke his arm trying to do some repairs to his old tractor."

"Do I need to come home?"

"We are good for now since the crops have been harvested. Gene helped a lot before he left for college. There's no need for either of you to come home right now. I just wanted you to know so you can pray for a quick healing. We might need you later on, if things take a while."

"I'd be glad to come. Work is slowing down at the factory. I'm not sure how long it will be before they start letting people go." He agreed Gene didn't need to interrupt his education. However, the urge to check on his folks was strong.

"Stay right where you are until you hear from us, son. Has anything been revealed by your searching yet?"

"Nothing, Ma. The basement's changed since we lived here."

"How 'bout a girlfriend?" Ma's question left Dale speechless.

He hesitated for a moment, trying to figure out a response. Ma's laughter sounded through the lines along with someone else's snickers. One of the gossiping cousins June mentioned must be listening in on their conversation.

"Look, Ma, I've got to get off before someone starts a rumor about our conversation. I'll answer your question when I find out myself. In the meantime, please keep me informed about how Papa Herbert's arm is healing." After saying goodbye he put the receiver back in its cradle and turned to see Miss Woodson grinning at him like she'd just gotten a Christmas present.

"I couldn't help overhearing part of your conversation. Is your stepfather going to be fine?" The woman's smiling face expressed curiosity, more than concern.

"I think he will be good with some rest." At least, Dale hoped so.

"Good. Maybe you'll have a surprising answer for your mother one of these days." Miss Woodson whisked by him and elbowed his side. Her cackles lingered in his ears as she sashayed back to her quarters.

Worries about Papa Herbert followed him through the next day at work.

"Is everything all right, Dale?" His usually grumpy supervisor paused as he held up a test tube to the light coming in from the window in their lab.

"I'm concerned about my step-pa. An accident broke Papa Herbert's arm yesterday."

Bob lowered the test tube into a holder. "Do you need some time off? I'm sure we could arrange a few days off since business has slowed down."

"I don't want to leave you hanging." Hopes of possibly going home made their way into Dale's mind.

"I'm sure one of the women who used to work here can step in if there's a need. With the reduction in production, finding a substitute probably won't be a concern. I wasn't going to say anything, but starting next week, the bosses are cutting us to three days a week. If you leave on a Friday night, you could come back by Wednesday morning. By taking those days off, you wouldn't miss any work. The factory doesn't even have to know you are gone. I'll work Monday through Wednesday. We'll overlap mid-week, and then you'll be on your own for Thursday and

Friday."

Relief poured into Dale's heart. If he rode an overnight train or bus, he could be home for a bit to check on his folks and see how they were really doing. "Thank you, sir."

"Don't mention it, and don't call me sir. I'm not military anymore. By the time you get back, I'll be starting on my art classes." A brief smile flitted across Bob's face as he began writing his findings on the required form. "Now, get busy. You're wasting time moping around like I did about checking into the G.I. Bill."

Dale fought the urge to salute and give the man another "yes, sir," but he closed his mouth. His thoughts whirled as he made plans to stop at either the bus or train station on the way home after work. Tomorrow was a Friday, so he'd have to make some quick plans. He'd let Miss Woodson know about his trip. Then his heart dropped. He would also need to delay his date with Betsy.

The rest of the afternoon dragged like a tired hound dog's tail. Wanting to go home waged a war with the desire to finally open the gates to a relationship with Betsy.

Once his workday was finished, Dale forced his steps toward the train depot and bus stop. After going both places, he returned to the train station and purchased a ticket. Visiting home was the right thing to do. His family mattered. He hoped Betsy would one day be part of the family, but for today he had made the best choice. With his ticket stuffed in his shirt pocket, he headed back to the boarding house.

Betsy sat on the porch's glider with her hands clasped together, her eyes anxiously focused on his as he approached. He reached toward her, and she took his offered hand.

"I'm sorry, Betsy. It looks like our date will have to wait until next weekend. I'm heading down to check on my folks tomorrow night. Ma insists she's doing fine since my Papa Herbert broke his arm, but I need to go check on them to make sure."

"I understand. I'd do the same thing if it were my mom or dad." Her beautiful face brightened his day.

Weights of worry and doubt fell from his shoulders. Relief poured into his chest as he sat next to her.

"Will you have to move back to the farm?" Betsy's voice sounded hesitant.

"I'm not planning on it at the moment, but I can't make any promises. Only God knows the future."

For a moment her expression changed to something he couldn't interpret. Then she smiled and patted his arm. "I hope your stepfather heals quickly. I will miss you."

"I have to be back to work by Wednesday, so you'll see me soon. Then we can make plans for the dessert I promised."

"Something sweet sounds wonderful." Her smile broadened and they pushed the glider into motion. "Tell me more about your family."

"Like I said before, since my brother died and Gene, the neighbor boy they took in, is starting college, there's just the three of us, Ma, Papa Herbert, and me. Mom stays busy with gardening and preserving food. Papa Herbert puts the meat on the table and takes care of the cash crops. We've got a few farm animals, some barn cats, and an old hound dog that lets us know when there's trouble or company around the place."

Betsy listened without talking. After a moment of silence, she seemed to be making a decision to speak. "I grew up on a farm too. I got a little tired of killing off chickens and canning beans." She chuckled. "I thought I'd escape doing farm chores by working for Miss Woodson. When the Depression and war came, she let the kitchen help go. I went back to my rural heritage afterward, to keep working at Woodson House. I'm not sure if I want to be a farm girl all my life."

"I'm hoping taking care of any chickens won't be in your future." He squirmed in the seat and made the glider swing crossways. He knew he couldn't promise her a farm-free future. At some point he would have to deal with his parents' heritage, either in person or from a distance. Maybe he was making a mistake to think about pursuing a relationship. There was a lot to think about.

"I guess I better go get my duffle packed for the weekend. The train pulls out right after work and gets back early Wednesday morning. I'll have to go straight to the factory after riding the train all night, but at least I can find out how bad things are at home. If I don't see you Wednesday morning, I'll be back here for supper in the evening."

He squeezed her hand and they walked side by side into the house.

Chapter Twenty-One

Scott
Present day, May

Scott sat side by side with his two favorite ladies. Scents of marinara sauce and garlic made their way through the restaurant. His stomach felt sated, but the last piece of pizza didn't need to go to waste. He and Melissa reached for the lone slice at the same time. Their hands connected. Scott laughed and waved toward the oozing cheese-covered triangle. "I think this piece is yours. There's no room in this stomach."

Melissa gasped and pulled away. "I'm sorry. You can have it." Her stammering voice shook. A tear glistened on her cheek in the flickering candlelight. The child's bottom lip quivered as she looked down at the red checkered tablecloth.

Ginny reached around the small table and hugged Melissa. Soothing music played in their ears as the two embraced. "Would you like to talk about what is upsetting you?" Scott placed a hand on each of their backs.

Melissa shook her head then nodded as her shoulders sank back into place. "One of Mom's boyfriends got mad when I took the last piece of pizza." She rubbed a scar on her forearm. "I didn't want Papa Scott to be mad at me."

Scott's heart sank as he leaned back in his seat. "I would never hurt you. As long as you are with us, you don't have to worry about either of us harming you." Ire at the man who left a mark on the child bubbled in his chest. He fought against clenching his fists, for fear Melissa would be frightened.

"But what if I make a mistake?" Her soulful gaze searched his face.

"Then we'll help you make a better choice. Everyone makes mistakes they can learn from, but we won't be leaving scars on your body to teach you a lesson." Ginny laid a hand on his wrist. Scott bit back other words he was tempted to say.

"Will I still be able to stay with you since Mama Ginny won't be teaching full-time next year? One time they took me away from my real mom because she didn't have a job."

Scott regretted their financial situation had become a source of worry for Melissa. Tonight's outing provided a consolation meal for the school levy failure. It would probably be the last restaurant visit for a while, since Scott and Ginny had already started discussing ways to tighten their budget.

"This family is good at pinching pennies. We'll find a way to keep you with us for as long as we can." He pulled a coin from his pocket and dropped it in her hand.

Melissa's frown slowly turned into a grin as she held the change between her thumb and finger. "I don't think I can pinch this penny."

"Exactly. You need to leave money matters up to the grownups who love you. Why don't you keep this money and start a piggy bank of your own?"

"What's a piggy bank?"

Scott pasted a smile on his face. The girl had missed out on so many little childhood traditions during her past. "It's a good way to save some money for something special. I created a homemade one out of a milk jug when I was a kid. I think it looked like a pig."

"Since I won't be working as much, I will have plenty of time to help you make a piggy bank just like Papa Scott's." Ginny's comment seemed to convey contentment about cutting back at work.

Dale
1946

The next day, Dale kept watching the time and hoping another shipment of goods wouldn't come in at the last second. Sometimes the work train ran earlier on Fridays due to the engineer cutting back his workweek. He prayed the freight wouldn't show up at the last minute and ruin his plans.

His supervisor laughed out loud. "Go ahead and leave for the depot. I know you were here early this morning. You've put in your hours, and your parents need you. I'll cover if the train shows up tonight. We're all caught up, so there may not be a need for more supplies."

"Thanks, Bob, I owe you." Dale grabbed his bag from under the worktable and bounded for the door.

Bob's laughter followed him, until the door slammed shut. The walk to the train station only took a few minutes. Dale checked his watch and then walked over to the blackboard with arrival times. There was plenty of time before his departure. After pacing the room for a few minutes, he sat down on a pew-like bench and closed his eyes in prayer. He'd been going full steam ahead ever since Ma's call. Praying hadn't been part of the rush. *Please, Lord, watch over Papa Herbert. I'm sorry he and I aren't in the best relationship. Help me to be a loving son. If possible, open up his heart to me.*

Peace and calm spread deep into his soul as he spent more time with the Lord. All too soon, the rumble and whistle of the train echoed through the depot while the engine slowed to a stop. As the building trembled, Dale roused from his prayers. Lifting his bag, he stepped onto the wooden platform and waited with several other people until the train completely stopped. Doors swept open, and conductors placed small steps between the platform and passenger car doorways.

Dale waved a hand to indicate a woman could go ahead of him. Then he made his way up the stairs and to a seat. Leaning back in the chair, he lifted his feet up onto the small metal footrest. He might as well get comfortable and try to rest. Maybe he could sleep some before he transferred trains in the middle of the night. He set his duffel on the seat beside him to discourage company and kept his eyes closed until the conductor came through the car to check tickets.

The following morning, Ma waited at the train depot, sitting high on the seat of an old farm wagon. The mules, Jenny and Jack, stood hitched into their traces as Ma held their reins. She had never learned to drive a motor car and didn't have any plans to get behind the wheel. Dale approached the team and rubbed the ears of the elderly mules.

One of these days, Ma would have to part with her faithful steeds. It would be a sad day. She'd been through so many things in her life. The loss of his father and brother wore heavily on her. He thanked the Lord Papa Herbert's accident only involved a broken arm. At least he would heal, and Ma's life as she knew it now would continue. He threw his bag in the back and clambered up next to Ma. Her embrace warmed him with the scents of fresh baking and home.

"It's good to see you, Ma." He gave her a tighter squeeze.

"I'm glad to see you too, though I said you didn't have to come." Her welcoming smile conveyed relief.

"There's no place I'd rather be right now." He took the reins when she offered them, clicked his tongue, and started the mules toward home. "There's no need to report to the powder plant until Wednesday. There's a cutback there. My supervisor worked it out for me to have a weekend with you. Besides, I'm sure I can find something to do around the old home place."

Ma sighed. "Thanks, I appreciate you taking the time to check on us." A sad expression crossed her face as she wove her fingers together. "I'm glad you came home alive from the war."

"I am too. I'm sorry about my brother. It should have been me. Maybe then your husband would be happier. His farming son would be here to cover for times like this." It was a good thing the mules knew their way home since his eyes seemed to glaze over with grief.

Ma swiped at her eyes. "We always tried to love you both equally. Herbert would have also been as upset if you were the one killed in action."

"Oh, Ma, I'm not his flesh and blood like my brother. There's been a divide ever since you gave birth to Joe."

Neither Dale nor his mother spoke for a while. The clip-clop of the mules' metal shoes on the road provided background noise during their break in conversation. Finally, he cleared his throat.

"I shouldn't have said anything. I respect and love you both. That's why I'm here. It's not like there's anything holding me back from staying."

Ma giggled. "Miss Woodson's letters hinted otherwise. It sounds like she's been doin' some matchmaking."

The change in subject brightened his spirits as he thought about his recent conversations with Betsy. "I reckon there might be a little interest from a couple of the ladies."

"Two ladies? How interestin'. I thought my former boss lady said her helper girl was the one you had your heart set on."

"You must know more than I do." He flicked the reins, making the mules pick up their pace. He couldn't control the smile spreading across his face. He heard more snickering from his mother as she ran her finger across his ears. She used to tease him about his ears turning red when he was embarrassed about something.

"You got something else you want to tell me, son?"

"I suppose I better fess up before you find anything else out from Miss Woodson. Betsy is pretty special. I've been hoping she'd go out with me. We sort of made plans for this weekend."

"Then what are you doing here?" Ma sounded indignant.

"She's a great gal and understands Pa's situation. I'm not sure she wants to go back to being a farm girl."

"Humph. There was a time I didn't want to live the country life either. That's when I up and married your pa during the war. I wanted to live a different type of life, which I did, thanks to Herbert and Miss Woodson. Losing your pa was terrible, but Miss Woodson made sure I would live to face each new day with purpose."

Betsy
1946

Betsy's thoughts warred within her mind. Did she want to follow her dream of living in the city? Or, would she purposely choose to go back to life on the farm? Dale's promise of a date sent warm feelings tingling from her head to her toes.

"Are you going to read the poem or daydream your day away?" Miss Woodson wiggled her eyebrows. "Are you missing Dale?"

Choosing not to answer, Betsy unfolded the poem and started reading as the older woman snickered.

A New Day

Once again, God has made all things new.
My husband, my love is gone to his reward.
His soul has found a resting place beyond this troubled world,
Where he can sing praises and remember happy times.

We placed his body beneath a sheltered grove with others long gone.
His stone relayed a brief listing of his accomplishments,
Those we can speak about, not those forever hidden,
In freedom seekers' hearts fleeing to another land.

The last few years brought changes to the man I loved.
He remained my Samuel and yet he wasn't.
Recollections came and went like shadows on a windy day,
Creating a different path for us both.

One that meandered like a twisting snail's trail,
Leaving behind evidence of drifting memories,
Fading into a stream of unknown presence,
Scattering bubbles of past events.

I stand and gaze up at the house that brought me to this place,
A wandering spirit, seeking to help and serve the ones I loved.
Many friends and travelers passed through this home,
As I waited for Samuel to make me his choice.

That day came and went too fast for us.
Our children filled this home with sweet devotion.
One child moved on, the other waits on the porch with arms open,
Ready to move forward, where few women have gone before.

Betsy wiped tears from her eyes as she shared the words with Miss Woodson. She stared at the family portrait hanging on one wall of the woman's quarters. The oil painting depicted a successful family, before changes came to the patriarch. The younger version of her employer displayed a powerful expression.

"She's talking about you in the last couple of lines, isn't she?"

"Yes. I loved my father, but his last few years about tore me to pieces. I didn't know what else to do except take over the production of the paper. At first, the men reporters were not happy with a woman in charge, but I didn't put up with their fussing.

"After all, we owned the paper and they didn't have much choice in the matter. By the time Father completely lost his abilities, I was on my own. Mother kept busy helping him with even the simplest chores, like shaving and taking care of basic needs. I think he enjoyed having her help him, though there were occasions where he even forgot her name. Not recognizing her probably hurt the worst, but she'd vowed to be with him through sickness and health, and that's what she did. Some friends tried to convince her to take him to an asylum. She said, 'absolutely not,' and from then on no one dared to pursue institutionalizing my father."

"She was an amazing woman." Betsy laid a hand on the other woman's arm.

Miss Woodson smiled. "I always admired her strength. Once Mother laid my Father Samuel to rest, she helped some at the paper but there was a change in her spirit. She seemed more interested in helping other elderly folks from our church and neighborhood. Mom even traveled to Canada to help her cousin during an illness, the one who at one time served her as a slave. My mother took on a new mission in life and left the newspaper business in my hands. I didn't mind at the time, but I've often wondered if my status as a powerful woman prevented me from having a beau."

The older woman turned toward her window and looked out onto the street running along the side of the house. A line of cars passed in front of the window. "I remember when this road consisted of a dusty path. Travelers rode on horses or in carriages. In my lifetime, mankind has gone from riding on animals to riding the wind in airplanes. I reported on every advance, every event, and ran our newspaper with finesse. Then I retired to my knitting and running this boarding house."

"But you still contribute to the paper." Betsy knew the woman's continued involvement to be a fact. She often took down her employer's words and entered them into type before delivering them to *The Gazette*. Miss Woodson may have turned management over to a new team of people, but she still liked to give them advice or write an editorial.

"So true, young lady, but what might have happened if I'd chosen a different path?" A frown marred her mostly smooth skin.

"Were you ever offered a chance with any gentleman callers?"

She snorted and looked back at Betsy. "There were several young men who expressed interest. It appeared they were more interested in courting the boss's daughter than really falling for me. Their eyes seemed to be set on inheriting the business."

"They missed out by not loving you for who you were." Betsy crossed her arms and leaned back into an embroidered chair near the window.

The older woman lifted a flowered handkerchief to the corner of one eye. "There was one fellow who might have been genuinely interested, but he spoke with a lisp. I'm afraid I wasn't very kind when he tried to get my attention. He was a fine man other than not having perfect diction. However, I was a stuck-up girl who wanted a guy with no imperfections. After a while he got my message and settled in with a much kinder woman than me. They both worked at *The Gazette* until they began having children. After several children arrived, he went to work for a bigger paper in Toledo to support his growing family."

"Do you ever hear anything about them?" Curiosity wove its way into Betsy's mind.

"I see him every Sunday at church. After retiring, he and his wife moved back to Forest Glen. She passed away a couple of years ago. He's always surrounded by a flock of grandchildren who appear to make him happy."

"Maybe you should invite them to eat here after church some Sunday." Betsy couldn't keep the excitement from her voice.

A dot of pink brushed the older woman's cheeks. "It is way too late for me to catch a fellow's eyes. You, my dear, are in a different place than me. Has Dale given you a hint about his feelings?"

"We've talked about going out, but since his stepfather's accident happened there hasn't been the occasion to do anything."

"Well, don't wait too long. He told me he would arrive back on Wednesday."

"I know, but there's always the issue of living in the country. You know I'm not thrilled about being a country girl again."

"I wasn't thrilled about a gentleman having a lisp either. When I look back, I wish I'd looked beyond his flaw and seen what a wonderful person he was. Besides, I don't think you were too impressed with city life when we took our trip."

Betsy nodded in agreement, hoping her cheeks were not coated with embarrassing color too.

"Maybe what you need is a compromise. I don't see Dale living in the country forever. He has his chemistry degree and will probably find a place to use his knowledge, like he is now at the factory in our town. You might find you can handle country life if there is a nearby town. You could even decide you want to have a family and take a few years to enjoy them without the stress of work."

"It sounds like you have us already married and preparing for children. He has only asked for one date." Betsy tried to frown at the older woman. Instead, she found her mouth muscles twitching into a smile.

"I've seen how he looks at you, though. If I'm not mistaken, your friendship has blossomed into something more serious." Miss Woodson's eyes seemed to twinkle as she winked at Betsy. "You should wear the pretty blue dress you bought in New York when we have dinner on

Wednesday evening. I happen to know he favors the color."

"Maybe I will, but only because you say I should. Now, I'm wondering if the gentleman who caught your eye might be a certain Mr. Sterling. You bought a rose-colored dress in the city when I bought mine. I think you should wear a pretty dress of your own to church next Sunday."

Both women burst into giggles, which slowly subsided. A sobering thought crossed Betsy's mind. What happened to the Woodson brother? She wasn't sure about voicing the question aloud, but decided to ask anyway, since they both broached subjects they'd avoided discussing.

"Was your brother ever interested in the paper?"

"Warren tried to show an interest, but his talent lay in woodworking. His heart wasn't in the written word. He enjoyed doing the physical part of running the press, which made Father happy for a while. Then he opened his carpenter's shop and created some of the furniture you see here in the house. He created the secretary's desk you are using. Remember, I'm leaving that writing table to you along with these poems. No one else in the family wants them. The desk wasn't one of his fancier pieces, though I always liked the hidden space for the typewriter. He made it for my use at the paper, so I can give it to whomever I want. If you visit my niece Lottie's home, you will see some of his better craftsmanship. I think she still has one of his baby cribs in her attic." Miss Woodson raised an eyebrow, hinting at something Betsy had no desire to explore.

"Thank you, the desk is an amazing gift." She'd always admired the end tables on either side of the niece's sofa when she'd carried a message to the woman's home. She decided not to ask about the crib.

"You earned it by working for room and board during the worst of the Depression years. I'm glad the future is brighter these days for a couple of my favorite boarders, you and Dale."

Betsy shrugged. "Is your brother still alive?"

"Warren passed away about fifteen years ago. His wife stayed at my niece's place for a few years afterward, but she soon entered heaven too. They both lived their faith with whole hearts and held the respect of everyone in town. Many homes still contain well-crafted examples of the furniture he created."

Chapter Twenty-Two

Ginny
Present Day, June

"Bye, Papa Scott. See you after your classes are over." Melissa waved as Scott headed off to the college. He'd opted to teach a full load of summer classes in addition to working afternoons as the department chair to help overcome their reduced income from the failed school levy.

"What are we going to do with school out?" Melissa dropped to the floor and played a game of tag with the dogs as Ginny scooped up a stack of empty tote bags.

"Kara and I need to sort teaching materials from our two rooms. We're job sharing next year, so we only need one set of everything."

"What does job sharing mean?" Melissa held a chew toy above Carlos's head, making the little dog dance in circles.

"Kara will teach in the morning before she goes to work at Amber Whitney's art store at noon. Then I will take over in the afternoon."

"But why do we have to bring stuff home?" The girl picked up the chihuahua and scratched behind his ears.

Ginny hugged Melissa as the small dog complained and wiggled out of their embrace. "I've got a lot of personal items and resources I need to remove from the classroom. There's even the rocking chair I've used for circle time." Ginny almost blurted out she would soon be putting the rocker to use in another way. Instead, she focused on the dogs bouncing around their feet. "We can display some of my basset hound statues on shelves around this house. The teaching supplies can be stored in the attic."

Melissa's eyes widened. "Cool. I've never explored an attic before. I wonder if there's a dragon's den up there like the one in the Woodson House."

"I have no idea. I haven't been up there yet. This house is ancient. I think it was built twenty or thirty years after the Woodson place."

"Wow, has Papa Scott said anything about what might be in the attic?"

"He said there was some old furniture and trunks. Maybe there's something we can refinish to use in your room or somewhere else down here. "

"All right, let's go get your Jezebel statues and hurry back." The girl rubbed noses with the dogs and headed for the front door.

A few hours later, Kara and Ginny's cars were full of boxes and totes. Kara pushed the trunk of her crammed car closed. "I hope there's enough room for you two ladies to squeeze into your car." She wiggled her eyebrows at Melissa, making the girl giggle.

"I'm sure we will find a way." Ginny hoped her words were true. At least there was only a short ride to endure the squish.

On the way home, their voices joined in song. Melissa's voice rang out even though her feet rested on a stack of bags, making her knees sit near her chin. When they pulled into the driveway, Carlos and Jezebel joined their howls to the music. One of the neighbors paused from working on a flower garden and shook her head before placing a finger on pursed lips.

Ginny and Melissa giggled, then carried armloads full of boxes and bags to the upstairs hallway. They left the rocker in the back seat of the car for Scott to unload later. After the last load, they collapsed on the front steps and sipped sodas.

"Can we explore the attic now?" Melissa pressed her hands together in a prayerful manner. Her eyes pleaded like a hound's.

Ginny snickered. "I see Jezebel's been teaching you how to beg."

"Is it working?" The child laced her fingers, pretending to pout.

"Let's go before you burst from curiosity." Ginny opened the door and led the way to the attic entrance. The small stairwell was dusty, but once they reached the top step, light from tiny windows on each end of the house made it bright enough to see where they were going. A single light bulb flared to life when Melissa pulled the chain. The space was bigger than Ginny imagined. A treasure trove of trunks, boxes, and furniture littered the upper room.

Melissa scuttled over to a small desk. "This would be perfect for my room or the study. I could use it for homework or drawing. I wouldn't have to use one of your desks."

"Then it is all yours."

"Forever?" The girl ran her fingers across the dusty top.

"Yes. I'm sorry things haven't worked out with your mother." Ginny's comment was an understatement. The last visitation had been a disaster. After the meeting with Melissa's mother, the case worker started working on the child's permanent removal to the care of Scott and Ginny. "It's only a matter of time before we can adopt you. Will you like being our beloved daughter, forever?"

Melissa threw her arms around Ginny. "Yes, Mama Ginny, I am so glad you love me." A moment later she rushed across the room. "Look, I think I found something for you." She pointed to an ornate wooden bassinet. "This is just what you need for my new sister or brother."

Ginny's mouth gaped open. "What? How did you know?"

The child smiled and waltzed away to explore other objects around the room. "The heat grates in this old house make wonderful listening devices."

They both laughed as Ginny explored the bassinet. The solid wood gleamed with a beautiful sheen, after she brushed grime from the little bed. She'd have to replace the mattress. She pulled the soiled padding from the bottom and stared in disbelief. Carved into the flat surface was W. Woodson. She tried to call out to Melissa, but dust filtering down her throat made it too scratchy to speak.

Dale
1946

A smattering of stars became visible in the chilly evening sky. Dale buttoned his jacket as he walked back from the little neighborhood market. He'd purchased some horehound in hopes the herb-based treat would help Miss Woodson with her scratchy throat. The candy provided a bitterly sweet home remedy his family enjoyed when they endured a cough or a hankering for a treat. The evening train growled its way through town and onto the side track for the powder plant. The thumps of the uncoupling process indicated they'd parked one car with tomorrow's chemicals. The next sound would soon be the train backing into the empty boxcar with a crashing noise to couple with it.

Boom, boom, boom.

The earth shook beneath his feet. Explosion after explosion drilled into his ears. The smell of rotten eggs and bananas filled the air. The chemicals of war were doing their worst. Smoke rose from the direction of the powder plant. A few windows cracked in a house nearby. Dale stuffed the bag of candy into his pocket and rushed toward the factory. Bells and sirens blared as he ran past Woodson House.

Several of the boarders waited on the porch, including Betsy. Relief edged into his heart when he saw his beautiful friend standing safely between June and Margie. He heard her calling, "Be careful," as he rushed past Woodson House. He was glad she cared. One day soon he'd let her know how much he loved her. They'd been dating since he returned from home and grew closer every day.

By the time he got near the plant, the police and fire department encircled the factory. With explosives involved, there was little they could do other than keep people back and let the chemicals burn out on their own. Dale turned his back on the scene and trudged toward Woodson House. The fire guaranteed the end of his employment at the powder plant.

He hoped the night watchman hadn't been anywhere near the

accident. No one else would have been there except for the one man, due to shutting down the evening shift a month ago. Chances were the guard dozed at the front gate until the explosion. Dale returned to the scene and mentioned the guard's name to one of the policemen, who assured him of the fellow's safety. Thank the Lord for the miracle.

As he neared the boarding house, Betsy ran to meet him and threw her arms around his shoulders. He drew her close and placed a kiss on her forehead. "It looks like everyone is safe."

"I'm just glad you weren't in the building when this happened." Tears streamed down her face.

"I am too. How is Woodson House? I saw one place with cracked windows." He lifted his eyes to survey the boarding house. Two windows on the front of the building bore scars of the explosion.

"We're all alive and well. Knowing everyone is safe is what matters. Windows and cracks can be replaced, people can't." Betsy linked her arm with his as they walked up the porch stairs.

An hour later, after assessing the cracked windows and walls on the upper floors of the house, Betsy and Dale made their way to the basement. The stovepipe had fallen from the wall connector, and the cement façade covering the older wall beneath revealed large cracks in several places. Before reconnecting the pipes, Dale held a flashlight up to the chimney hole and looked into the hollow space below.

"It looks like an old-fashioned fireplace inside this cavity." He pried at one of the cracked pieces on the wall, and it fell with a crash to the floor, revealing a stone wall behind it. "Do you know where Miss Woodson might have a screwdriver or a chisel? I'm going to take off this cement cover and get a look at what's behind it. I think the secret room might be here."

Betsy ran into the other room, and he heard metal tools clanging together. Moments later she returned with several implements in her arms. "These look like they might work."

"Perfect." He paused. "We should go ask permission from Miss Woodson before we do this." They walked to the top of the stairs and found the homeowner waiting for them.

"We think we may know where the secret room is." Betsy's voice brimmed with excitement as she rocked from one foot to the other.

Dale laid a calming hand on her back and focused on Miss Woodson. "May we have your permission to pry some of the cement off the walls in the furnace room? Right now, we can see the original stone wall underneath. If you allow, we'd like to see if there's an opening to the hidden place."

Miss Woodson rubbed her hands together. "You may, if you let me be part of your treasure hunt. I was once a brave young woman, but I've let my childhood fears keep me from adventures in my old age. Today I'm going to change. Help me down these stairs. I want to face the dragon in its den."

The younger couple each held an arm and assisted the older woman down into the basement. Betsy dusted off an old stool for Miss Woodson to sit upon and observe the process. Dale carefully chipped away at the layer of cement. Betsy carted the pieces out the basement door and stacked them on the sidewalk outside.

When she grew tired, they switched jobs, and she took her turn removing the gray coat covering the tan river stones. Dale didn't mind the opportunity to step out into the fresh air to cart away the slabs of cement. All three shared pieces of horehound candy when effects from the dust made them cough and sneeze. Hours later, the revealed wall of original rocks filled one side of the room.

"I like it better than the old cement, but where is our treasure room?" Miss Woodson looked from the stones to the couple in front of her.

Something stirred in Dale's memories. "I think I remember leaning on the wall and falling backward into darkness." He started pushing a section of the wall. Nothing happened.

Betsy leaned next to him, pushing on a lower section of rocks. A small crack opened in the wall and then movement stopped.

"It looks like you might have found something." Miss Woodson clapped her hands.

"I wonder why it didn't open for me." Dale scratched his head.

"You were a little shorter back then. We could sure use the strength you have now. I can't get it to move." Betsy groaned as she tried to push the opening farther in. Dale offered her a hand to help her stand. Her nearness shot a spark of awareness through him, distracting him from his goal. After a few seconds, he stepped away and looked at the opening she'd made in the wall. He sat down on his knees and pushed with every ounce of strength he could muster. Finally, a low doorway opened, revealing a thin room off to the side, built between two walls of stone.

"Hand me the flashlight, Betsy." Their hands brushed as he grasped the light, reigniting the hope in his soul. Someday he wanted to marry her. A wedding couldn't happen soon with his work literally going up in smoke. He concentrated on the task at hand and pointed the light into the chamber. Sure enough, a dusty Whitman's box sat on a small ledge in the space. A tiny wooden soldier lay next to the box. A memory of holding the toy flashed through his mind. He grasped the box and the plaything as he edged out of the space. "I don't think I'd fit very well if I were a runaway back in slavery days."

Miss Woodson leaned closer. "From the tales my mother told, the people were pretty thin by the time they got here. Hiding in there wouldn't have been much of a problem. May I see?"

Betsy helped the older woman slide down to her knees so she could peer into the little room. "I think we've discovered a national treasure here. I have a circle of historically minded friends who may want to make something of our discovery one day." Miss Woodson's smile spread across her face as they helped her back onto her stool.

"Speaking of treasures, did you open your mother's Whitman's box yet?" Betsy's gaze looked at the container and soldier in Dale's hands. He suddenly felt unsure about opening his mother's precious things in front of others. What if it revealed something embarrassing? Then he looked into Betsy's face and knew whatever lay hidden in the box, he wanted to share it with her. It didn't matter whether it held good or bad, he hoped she'd be part of his future.

He handed the little soldier to Betsy and looked deeply into her eyes as he wrapped his fingers around hers and the toy. "I'm looking at my best treasure right now."

Miss Woodson giggled in the background. He held Betsy's hand for a moment more, before releasing it and edging the lid from the Whitman's Chocolate sampler. It took him a moment for his mind to comprehend what he saw. Purple ribbon attached to a military medal sat in one section of the box. Awe wove through his mind as he remembered his father's ultimate gift to the country. Then, another glittering object caught his attention. A gold chain looped its way through the little cubicles where chocolate once lay. Within its length, a pair of golden bands and a matching diamond ring dangled.

"These must have been my parents' wedding rings!" He threw caution to the wind as he knelt on the dusty basement floor and looked into Betsy's cement-smudged face. "I don't have a job right now, so we will have a long engagement before we can marry. I do have my mother's rings. Will you marry me in the future, even if we end up living on the farm?"

A teasing glint came to Betsy's eyes. Dale squirmed in the dust at her feet. He looked up at her and hoped she saw the plea in his heart. "Betsy?"

"Let me think for a moment. I happen to have a pretty good position here with Miss Woodson. I hear she might be in need of a handyman to do some work in her basement since she has a newly destroyed wall. Home repairs might keep you busy until they restore the factory, or a better job comes along for you. Maybe we could get married sooner and move into the room over the kitchen. Did you know Paul and Ellen are moving into their own place next week?"

Dale's heartbeat thumped in his chest. "So are you saying yes, even if we have to move back to the farm at some point?"

"Yes, Dale, I will marry you. A farm sounds like a good place to raise a little girl or boy someday." She held out her hand with the little soldier resting in her hand. "Can I have my Whitman's treasure now?" He pocketed the soldier and brushed his lips across her palm. Then he removed the diamond ring from the chain. As he placed it on her finger, he rose and kissed her soft lips, sharing his deep love.

Epilogue

Ginny
Present day, several months later

Scott's kiss sent a wave of happiness into Ginny's heart. They had gathered outside the courthouse where their early morning adoption of Melissa would take place within the hour. They'd paused on the steps for a final hug. Roy and her mother walked ahead of them toward the building, hand in hand with Ginny and Scott's future daughter. Honey, Hope, Loretta, Annabelle, and her friend Annie from the historical museum had joined them for the celebration taking place shortly. Scott's parents hurried up the stairs and waved to the group. This would be Ginny and Scott's last few moments as a couple without children. In an hour they'd officially be a family of three. A cramping pain made its way across Ginny's back. She groaned. Maybe she should say a family of four. She'd been feeling some discomfort since waking up.

"Are you all right?" Scott wrapped his arm around her as the deep ache washed over her mid-section and then subsided.

She laughed. "I will be, but I think we better head into the courthouse and get our Melissa adopted as soon as possible."

"Is it time?" Her husband's face turned pale as he danced from side to side, grasping her elbow.

Ginny patted his arm. "We have a while, so no need to panic. Last week, the doctor assured me our baby is healthy and strong. I do have a feeling Melissa will be spending tonight with her new grandma and grandpa while we head for the hospital. It looks like our hopes for a family are all being fulfilled within one day."

An hour later they walked out of the courthouse, holding their daughter's hands and making plans for their start as a growing family-- once baby Treasure Hope arrived.

END

THANK YOU!

Thank you for reading this book from Mt. Zion Ridge Press.

If you enjoyed the experience, learned something, gained a new perspective, or made new friends through story, could you do us a favor and write a review on Goodreads or wherever you bought the book?

Thanks! We and our authors appreciate it.

We invite you to visit our website: *www.MtZionRidgePress.com* and explore other titles in fiction and non-fiction. We always have something coming up that's new and off the beaten path.

And please check out our podcast, **Books on the Ridge,** where we chat with our authors and give them a chance to share what was in their hearts while they wrote their book, as well as fun anecdotes and glimpses into their lives and experiences and the writing process. And we always discuss a very important topic: *Tea!*

You can listen to the podcast on our website or find it at most of the usual places where podcasts are available online. Please subscribe so you don't miss a single episode!

Thanks for reading. We hope to see you again soon!

About the Author

Bettie Boswell always loved to read and create stories for church, family, and friends. In 2016 she began writing and illustrating stories to share with the world. She is now an author/illustrator of both children's and Christian adult fiction and non-fiction books. Her efforts include contributions to educational works, leveled readers, magazine articles, and devotional and short story anthologies. Bettie has two grown sons, one daughter-in-law, three grandchildren, and a busy minister husband.

https://sites.google.com/view/bettieboswellauthorillustrator/home